MVFOL

What had come over her?

Her heated reference to "the lady in question" had carried the blatant insinuation that he was setting up a mistress.

"I apologize," she said stiffly. "I had no right to make any assumptions."

"No, you didn't," Richard Miles agreed lightly. "Although I suppose a bit of fishing in the interest of gratifying your feminine curiosity was too much to resist."

"I wasn't fishing," Julia replied, infuriated all over again that he was acting so contrary to her expectations. "And it was not curiosity," she denied belligerently.

"Interest then," he amended carelessly.

Julia held his wry gaze stonily. "Nothing about you interests me," she said with commendable frost.

"I could change that, Julia," he murmured with silky-soft menace.

D0249831

EDWINA SHORE spent thirteen years working in Australia's publishing community, editing mainly academic work, with a few brief forays into general trade or "bestseller" publishing. Now, when she isn't immersed in her own writing, she tries to work on her other interests, which include travel to Great Britain, Europe and throughout Australia, learning Scottish Gaelic, sculpting and painting. She is single and lives in Victoria.

Books by Edwina Shore

HARLEQUIN PRESENTS
1172—JUST ANOTHER MARRIED MAN

HARLEQUIN ROMANCE
2753—A WILL TO LOVE
2798—THE LAST BARRIER
2946—A NOT-SO-PERFECT MARRIAGE
2962—STORM CLOUDS GATHERING

Don't miss any of our special offers. Write to us at the following address for information on our newest releases.

Harlequin Reader Service
P.O. Box 1397, Buffalo, NY 14240
Canadian address: P.O. Box 603,
Fort Erie, Ont. L2A 5X3

EDWINA SHORE

not his property

Harlequin Books

TORONTO • NEW YORK • LONDON
AMSTERDAM • PARIS • SYDNEY • HAMBURG
STOCKHOLM • ATHENS • TOKYO • MILAN

Harlequin Presents first edition February 1992
ISBN 0-373-11437-0

Original hardcover edition published in 1990
by Mills & Boon Limited

NOT HIS PROPERTY

Copyright © 1990 by Edwina Shore. All rights reserved.
Except for use in any review, the reproduction or utilization
of this work in whole or in part in any form by any electronic,
mechanical or other means, now known or hereafter invented,
including xerography, photocopying and recording,
or in any information storage or retrieval system, is forbidden without
the permission of the publisher, Harlequin Enterprises Limited,
225 Duncan Mill Road, Don Mills, Ontario, Canada M3B 3K9.

All the characters in this book have no existence outside the
imagination of the author and have no relation whatsoever to
anyone bearing the same name or names. They are not even
distantly inspired by any individual known or unknown to the
author, and all incidents are pure invention.

® are Trademarks registered in the United States Patent and
Trademark Office and in other countries.

Printed in U.S.A.

CHAPTER ONE

SUZIE had put him through as 'Mr Miles, interested in the Chiswell Mews place,' but the first thing that struck Julia about the clipped, impatient voice enquiring about the rather cutesie-pie property was that it didn't sound as if it belonged to what she called a 'mews type'; six years of dealing with people who bought and sold mews properties—as well as owning one herself—had made her into something of an expert on the subject, and in her book Mr Miles and mews just did not go together.

'No, I want to view the property today and suggest we meet there in an hour,' he cut through her offer of an appointment for the next day, the peremptory voice not so much suggesting as ordering, it sounded to Julia,. and it was with distinct frost in her own voice that she explained that Dawlish's company policy required all prospective clients, buyers and sellers alike, to come into the office in the first instance, and no, neither she nor anybody else from the office would meet him off the premises as he was 'suggesting'. Julia underscored his word with piqued emphasis, and then thought the ensuing silence from Mr Miles's end meant he was about to snap a 'forget it' and hang up on her, and, quite frankly, she would have considered it a favour.

'A very commendable policy,' Mr Miles returned after the prolonged pause, an unseen dry smile in the contrary approval giving Julia the feeling he was patting her on the head. 'In which case. . . Miss Radcliffe, isn't it. . .may I suggest I come to your office at two o'clock—if that's convenient to you?' In an about-turn, he was laying on the courtesy and charm with a trowel, and without the hop-to-it edge the voice was very attractive, Julia noted, remaining utterly unimpressed by its owner.

'Two o'clock will be fine, Mr Miles,' she agreed frostily, hung up and groaned aloud out of sheer frustration.

The last thing she needed was an interruption to her afternoon—her last afternoon. . .last day, at Dawlish and thank heavens for that, but there was still so much she felt obliged to sort through, check, and tidy up that she had already intended working through her lunch hour to be able to leave with Moira at five for the farewell drink and early dinner to which the office administrator insisted on treating her, since Jeremy Dawlish hadn't thought to organise any sort of official office send-off. Now, with the prospect of at least an hour out of her afternoon, there wasn't much chance of finishing by five.

Moira would wait, of course, but it would be a nuisance to have their plan upset by the insistent Mr Miles wanting to view a property which Julia found hard to believe could possibly be of genuine interest to him. And par for the course that she was the only one around to take him to see it, because, her last day or no, Jeremy had taken himself off with girl-friend-cum-new negotiator, Deborah, for one of their interminable lunches which started around noon and went on for most of the afternoon, and Julia doubted they would even bother to come back to say goodbye to her.

That hurt, whatever she told herself. . .that she didn't care, that she'd had enough of Jeremy and Dawlish and never wanted to see either again. . .that she regretted waiting this long finally to walk out of the door when the writing had been on the wall a year ago, if only her misguided sense of loyalty hadn't got in the way of her reading it. And look where that loyalty had got her—precisely nowhere, and in a perverse sort of way her boss not bothering to even say 'thanks and good luck' was a fitting ending to what had started out as a fabulous career and turned into something that made her not want to leave her bed in the mornings to face the day.

Well, the last rat was deserting the sinking ship, and not before time, Julia cheered herself grimly, bringing out the contents of one of the drawers of the filing cabinet and wondering why she should care about leaving everything ship-shape when no one else would, least of all Jeremy Dawlish. Professional pride, she supposed—or what the last dispiriting year had left of it. She spread the files over the desk and gave a glance at her watch as she sat down; just on one o'clock, and then the next time she threw a startled glance at it was at twenty to two when Mr Miles walked in, unannounced, because Suzie was still at lunch, and catching Julia off guard, files scattered all over the place and mouth full of the salmon sandwich Suzie had brought in before heading off to her own lunch and leaving Reception temporarily unattended.

There was always someone in one of the offices

during the lunch hour, though—Julia today, and the buzzer on the front desk had a sign alongside: 'Please press if desk unattended,' which was what most people did. Not Mr Miles, it seemed, and Julia knew instinctively that the tall, dark man in the navy pin-striped suit was the owner of the voice that snapped and charmed in alternate breaths; his strolling into her office as if he owned the place was merely a by-the-by confirmation of the sour impression left by his telephone call—that casual arrogance was second nature to him.

Julia swallowed her mouthful with the startled glance at her watch, scooped the remainder of the half-eaten sandwich into the top drawer and swept most of the files to the side of the desk, all in pretty much the same agitated movement as jumping to her feet, furious at the arrogant intrusion and flaring scarlet to the roots of her red hair at having been caught by a client chomping inelegantly on a sand-wich in the midst of what must have looked like the messiest, most unprofessional office in the whole of London. If he'd caught her prancing naked around the office, Julia could not have been more embarrassed.

'Miss Radcliffe. . . Richard Miles,' he introduced himself in the instantly recognisable voice—the charming version of it. 'I'm afraid I'm a little early. There was no one at the desk and I noticed your name on the door. I hope I'm not interrupting anything important,' he added, apologetically, but with what looked suspiciously like amusement gleaming in the darkly lashed brown eyes as they took in her desk, her fluster and embarrassment, and then, as Julia just stood there, continued taking her in in a leisurely appraisal that was too obviously appreciative and—no bones about it—pure impertinence, and it got her moving at last on a wave of tightly suppressed hostility.

Given the circumstances, she felt the smile was a credit to her. . .distant, brief, and as professional as her extended hand as she came briskly around the old wooden desk. 'Mr Miles; how do you do?' Julia bit the words out in icy staccato, offering no explanation or apology for the debris, nor the overpowering waft of salmon floating about the small, badly ventilated office.

She had her hand in and out of his in a quick, practised twist, perfected over years of extricating it out of male hands that clasped too long and too intimately, although to give Richard Miles his due— grudgingly—there was nothing about his cool, firm handshake that even she could object to, but that was probably only because she had surprised him into it. She didn't miss the reassessing flicker in dark chocolate eyes as she met them briefly in bland, professional contact.

Not a man used to women taking the initiative in business dealings, she summed him up tartly, gesturing towards the chair in front of her desk. 'Do sit down, won't you?' Her poise recovered, she was taking belated control of the interview, a shade officiously perhaps, in overcompensation for those first flustered moments, only Richard Miles didn't make any move towards the chair, and instantly, with a renewed charge of hostility, Julia took that as a challenge to her attempt to establish control. 'Sit down, please, Mr Miles,' she ordered with almost schoolmarmish firmness. 'I need to take down a few details.'

'I was under the impression you just had, Miss Radcliffe—taken in a few details, if not actually down. Come, come,' he chided with a sardonic smile as Julia frowned her incomprehension. 'Isn't the aim of forcing people into the office—the men, at least— to check out that they're not Jack the Ripper?'

What he said was basically true, and most estate agencies had taken up the practice in recent times, although the point of the cautionary exercise was somewhat defeated in this instance, because if Richard Miles had been Jack the Ripper she would have been no safer here in the temporarily deserted office than in the empty house in Chiswell Mews.

'I'm right, aren't I?' The irritating sardonic smile continued when she couldn't deny his interpretation of the company's safety-net policy. 'And a very wise precaution in the case of such an attractive woman as yourself, I grant you, Miss Radcliffe,' he put in suavely, and Julia felt a new surge of heat into her cheeks at the gratuitous flattery which she suspected was inserted deliberately to annoy her. 'But now that you've reassured yourself about me—you *have* reassured yourself, haven't you?' he added with spurious concern. 'Perhaps we could dispense with the time-wasting charade of taking down my life story and go to view the property I've come to see.' The tone was bantering, and the eyes still held that gleam of amusement, but all the same Julia had the sense that he was testing her—baiting her, more like.

'I'm afraid I must adhere to company policy, Mr

Miles.' She stuck to her guns with an excess of politeness. 'However, since you're so very obviously pressed for time, may I suggest you make an appointment for another day? One day next week, perhaps?' she offered, ultra-helpfully, as she held the sardonic gaze in a cool stare of her own, and then, while he didn't actually shrug as such, she read the 'oh, why not?' in the deliberately languid move to the chair. Point to her, but she would much rather have lost it, seen the back of him and got on with her files. She couldn't remember when she had last felt such instant antagonism towards a client, and heaven only knew she'd come across more than her fair share of men who couldn't go through a simple business encounter with an attractive woman without trying to turn it into some sort of showcase for their egos. Usually she coped with them with cool professionalism; today, she wasn't sure she was up to it.

Richard Miles settled himself into the worn leather chair and leaned back in it, casually, as if it were his office, not hers. 'I'm ready to divulge all, Miss Radcliffe.' Humouring her, damn it, voice and smile both, and with something in the eyes that sent her hand flying up to do an involuntary lightning check of the top buttons of her cream silk shirt as she returned hastily to her side of the desk.

The buttons were done up. Julia sat down, her cheeks dreadfully hot again, their translucent creaminess bright scarlet. The bane of her life, that blush; it was so childish and so appallingly unprofessional, and the prolonged riffling through the scatter of files was not exactly adding to her image either.

Folder finally unearthed, Julia took out one of the

photocopied forms Dawlish used for taking client particulars. Nothing overly personal. . .name, address, type of property preferred. . .price range— all perfectly legitimate questions, and never in all her time with Dawlish had she ever felt embarrassed about asking them. And yet, irrationally, Julia felt embarrassed now—as if the questions would be construed as interest or curiosity on her part. Absurd, because she did not have the slightest interest or curiosity about Mr Miles. Ask them and get it over with, she ordered herself, flicking back a wayward strand of the shoulder-length hair that had swung across one cheek. She picked up her pen and wrote 'Richard Miles' against 'name', then, ignoring her own order, ran her eyes down the form, skipping over all the other questions until she came to 'type of property preferred'.

She lifted her head at last and looked him full in the face. A very handsome face, she had to admit with an unwilling, hostile appreciation of the emphatically defined features. . .the sweep of heavy black brows that went with the almost black hair and the thick, dark lashes she would have killed for. The nose was strong and straight, the jawline hard-edged, and, although there were incongruous little upward tilts at the corners of the firm mouth, overall it was an uncompromisingly masculine face, and the man himself one of those too self-assured, too male types she had never felt comfortable with even when she didn't dislike them on sight. Richard Miles in a pritzy little mews house? Her imagination couldn't stretch to it, yet ostensibly he was so interested in that house he had shot over twenty minutes early. Couldn't wait to see it, in fact.

Julia suddenly became aware that one of the thick black brows was hoisted up quizzically and that Richard Miles was looking back at her with a small twist of a smile playing around those incongruously uptilted corners of his mouth. She had been staring— blatantly. 'Any other type of property—aside from Chiswell Mews, Mr Miles?' she asked hastily. 'It is Chiswell Mews you're interested in?' The second question came over as a challenge.

'The Chiswell Mews property, Miss Radcliffe, nothing else,' Richard Miles confirmed blandly, offering no elaboration of his interest, and Julia could have kicked herself for the out-of-the-blue spurt of pure, feminine curiosity.

For a daughter? She tossed the notion aside—too young. . .he didn't look more than thirty-two or -three. Ex-wife? An investment? Girlfriend. . .? Of course, girlfriend, she concluded acidly; he was just the type to set up a girlfriend in a cute little mews. Dropping her eyes to the form again, she wrote in 'Chiswell Mews only' and slipped the form back into the folder.

'Is that all?' Richard Miles affected surprised disappointment. 'Hardly worth sitting down for, was it? Except to prove a point, of course,' he added slyly. 'But are you sure there isn't anything else you would like to know about me?' The voice was a silken, intimate purr—obviously his idea of fatuous humour, but it was unnerving that it could produce the funny little tingle down her spine.

Julia flicked him a tightly controlled glance. 'Quite

sure,' she snapped. 'Well, yes: your telephone number,' she muttered in a change of mind on the off chance that someone in the office might want to follow him up after she was gone, and was just finishing jotting the number he gave when, to her relief, she heard sounds in the front office. Jeremy and Deborah? You never knew your luck, and she might be able to palm off Richard Miles on one of them yet. She stood up. 'I'm sure you'd like to see the property now,' she said briskly.

'Dying to,' he agreed drily, easing himself out of the chair and watching her reach for her jacket hanging on the side of the filing cabinet, but making no move to try to help her into it, possibly because he'd read the warding-off message in her quick glare, although more likely to better enjoy the view of her rather ungainly scramble into the jacket. What was it about the man that had her behaving like an adolescent in the first flush of sexual awareness, thrown into idiotic coyness because he could see the outline of her lacy slip under the light silk of the shirt?

Jacket on and buttoned up, Julia took her handbag out of the bottom drawer of the desk and led the way out of the room and into the front office, where her heart sank to see her luck was still well and truly out that day and it was only Suzie back from lunch.

She went over to the low cupboard at the side of Suzie's desk and took a set of keys off the board attached to the inside of the cupboard door. 'I'm taking Mr Miles to view the Chiswell Mews property,' she told Suzie in a terse aside, and doubted if the young receptionist heard a word. Suzie had her eyes glued on Richard Miles, who in turn appeared

more interested in his intent survey of the office than
in Suzie's bat-eyed interest in him, and momentarily
Julia saw the office through those sharp brown eyes
and winced for Dawlish. . .shabby and old-
fashioned, everything wooden and worn, whereas
everything about Richard Miles spoke eloquently of
another world: sophisticated. . .modern. Moneyed.
Whatever his occupation, and she hadn't dreamt of
asking, it was obviously practised in surroundings
light-years removed from the 'seen better days' of
Dawlish.

'If you wouldn't mind waiting here a few minutes,
I'll bring the car around to the front door.' Leaving
him to his inspection, Julia walked past him and was
swinging the glass front door open when he came up
behind her.

'I'll come along with you,' he invited himself.

'As you wish,' she replied shortly as he fell into
step beside her angry stride down the footpath. It
certainly was not what she wished—as if he hadn't
guessed she didn't want an audience while she got
the car out.

I was parked behind the building, and to get to it
they went through an archway into a mews at the
end of a row of shops, then turned right into a lane
of sorts that ran along behind the first dozen or so of
the shops and offices that fronted the main street.
The short walk, at the pace of a route-march, was in
total silence with neither of them volunteering a
word.

Dawlish had four spaces of parking in the small,
private parking area—worth the proverbial king's
ransom in this pocket of the West End. Julia had

parked her small Peugeot that came with the job behind Moira's aged Morris, and then it seemed that Deborah Purton had arrived and rammed her nifty, non-company Triumph against the bumper of Julia's car, leaving yards of room for herself to back out and never mind she hadn't left any for the hapless person in front. Jeremy's girlfriend was not known for her consideration. Julia took in the *déjà-vu* scene at an angry glance, then stonily unlocked the passenger door.

'Would you like me to get it out for you?' Richard Miles offered helpfully, suppressing the small smile—but not quickly enough—that put paid to any chance of Julia accepting the offer.

'No, thank you,' she shot back grimly, and didn't miss the smirk as he got into his seat.

She was a good driver and had got herself out of tight spots before, and in ordinary circumstances would have got out now—with difficulty, granted, and a lot of dark muttering, if not actual swearing, about Ms Purton. With Richard Miles sitting in what she took to be smug silence beside her, Julia couldn't even give vent to her frustration with a few choice 'damns' and 'blasts' as she manoeuvred the wheels this way and that, backing and froing until her shoulders ached and perspiration sprang to her forehead.

'Hop out,' he ordered suddenly. 'For Pete's sake, we'll be here all afternoon!' He was out of the car before Julia could protest, and around her side in a couple of strides, and then she had the choice of digging her heels in and refusing to budge, or admitting defeat and letting him try to get the car out.

She climbed out ungraciously, and then, naturally, he managed to make it look child's play as he swung the vehicle out in a few expert twists of the wheels—all she needed to make her feel a complete idiot.

'Thank you,' she muttered when they returned to their respective places.

'Not at all. My pleasure.'

The mock gallantry made Julia grind her teeth as she drove them down the lane and out of the mews.

'A nuisance, this driving clients about, isn't it? One of the drawbacks of working in real estate, or so I would imagine.'

He was making conversation. It was her job to do that, and she had fallen down on it disgracefully. Last day at Dawlish, and, uptight as she was, she owed her professionalism, if not Richard Miles, at least a token effort. Julia flicked her eyes off the road for an instant to flash him a brief glance. 'I don't usually mind,' she replied, and was immediately conscious of the way the emphasis had inadvertently fallen on the word 'usually'. Inadvertently. . .? 'I mean——'

'You mean you just mind driving me around,' he cut off her attempt to backtrack with a dry laugh.

'Don't be ridiculous, Mr Miles, of course I don't,' Julia lied crossly, chagrined that her antagonism towards him had been so transparent.

'Of course you don't,' he shot back softly. 'However did I come to think of it?'

Uncomfortable and angry, Julia kept her mouth clamped shut and her eyes fixedly ahead, not knowing what to say any more to the disconcerting man beside her. Usually she found conversation with a client easy, not to say necessary; it gave her the chance to establish a rapport and at the same time get a better overall picture to help her place them into the right property. The trouble was, it had taken her all of about two seconds to get an overall picture of what Mr Miles was all about, and she didn't like it. . .didn't like the way he looked at her through those preposterously long and enviably dark lashes. . .didn't like the way his voice could turn disturbingly intimate—deliberately, to unnerve her—nor the way he seemed to find her barely suppressed antagonism amusing. No, she did not like Richard Miles one bit, but that was no excuse for her lapse of professionalism.

Julia concentrated on the traffic and hoped he took it as the reason for the silence that was, for her at any rate, thick with tension, and when she finally turned into Chiswell Mews to cruise slowly over the cobblestones it wasn't soon enough.

'Here we are,' she announced with jarring brightness as she came to the tiny house with the brilliant yellow door. 'There's no "For Sale" board because the owner requested we didn't put one up. He feels they mar the look of a place,' she explained, then waited for Richard Miles to hop out before parking the car flush against the garage door.

He barely gave the house a glance as Julia unlocked the front door and let them in, then, lost cause or no, determinedly went into 'selling mode', taking him first into the garage which took up most of the ground level, and pointing out the sizeable store-room at the back, together with the obvious advantage of having a garage in an area where street parking was impossible. Richard looked everywhere she pointed, did a lot of silent, solemn nodding and made her feel he was as much role-playing the prospective buyer as she was the professional negotiator. Just as she had figured, he was not the slightest bit interested, she concluded on a note of sour self-congratulation that she had taken his measure so accurately from the moment she had heard his voice over the telephone.

She led them back into the main part of the house where the owner, a young man of ambivalent persuasion, had gone to a lot of trouble—expense too— in creating his perfect environment. Richard tossed a glance at the enormous gilt mirror reflecting the tiny hall, up at the chandelier that would have done a *palazzo* proud, and grimaced. His first real reaction— for what it was worth, noted Julia tartly as she started leading the way up the steep, narrow stairs, carpeted in soft, beigey pink with the walls a lighter tone and abounding in prints in gilt frames.

He was right behind her and she was never more conscious of the slimness of her skirt, nor of the way she needed to sway her hips with each high step, and all the time, she could feel his eyes burning into her back until it was all she could do to stop herself from swinging around to tell him to stop ogling. High steps and high heels notwithstanding, she fairly galloped up the last couple of steps, spinning around with a red-faced glare when she reached the landing, only to see him intently—innocently—examining one of the prints way down the staircase, and then she nearly burst out laughing at herself and the absurd projections of her imagination gone quite mad.

'You'll notice the skylight gives the staircase so much extra light,' she pointed out when he joined her on the landing, and gave him a really warm smile as a sort of silent apology for having implied, albeit only mentally, that he was a raging lecher.

'So it does,' he agreed without looking up, seemingly more interested in her smile than the skylight. Granted, it was the first genuine one she had given him, but did he have to look as if she had just propositioned him and he was considering the offer. . .?

Julia flicked her smile off in a hurry. 'Yes, well. . .' she said tersely, and swung away so abruptly she banged into the wall in her haste to try and move them off the tiny, claustrophobic landing which had them standing so close they might have been about to dance.

Richard shot out a hand to steady her. 'Whoa, Miss Radcliffe, you'll do yourself an injury—or knock a hole in the wall,' he admonished her with a laugh. 'And I thought you'd quite reassured yourself I wasn't Jack the Ripper.'

'Very funny,' Julia retorted snappishly. 'Now please let go of my arm, Mr Miles.' She tried to dislodge his grip with an angry jerk of her arm.

'Only if you're sure you won't fall over in alarm at standing so close to me,' he returned in the silky purr that she hated, but did as she ordered and released her. 'Are you always so nervous of your male clients, Miss Radcliffe, or just me?'

Julia's only answer to that was a cold stare. She

flung open one of the three doors on the landing. 'The main bedroom,' she muttered, and speedily manoeuvred herself away from the doorway so she was standing behind him as he glanced in—barely. 'And this is the bathroom.' She opened another door.

Richard did not bother to look in. 'I'll take your word for it,' he said carelessly as he followed her into the main living area which had kitchen and dining facilities at one end and sitting-room at the other, with a door at that end giving into a second, tiny bedroom—very much the same set-up as in her own place and in most small mews houses, although this owner's singular taste in furnishings was all his own, and the quantity no less astonishing.

With so much crammed into so little, Julia briskly started on the clever utilisation of limited space, and wondered why she was wasting her breath. Richard Miles gave the room a cursory, uninterested glance, forgetting even to nod solemnly. And she had been dragged out of the office on her last day for this? An utterly bored non-client who was more interested in playing silly macho games than in the house he supposedly hadn't been able to wait to see. Julia checked her tongue, but managed the feat only for an instant.

'You're just not interested, are you, Mr Miles?' she challenged outright at last, his attitude too much to take a moment longer, and her own tension and irritation demanding release.

Richard Miles didn't blink. 'Why do you say that?' he enquired politely.

Julia made an angry grating sound, a cross between

a laugh and a snort. 'Because, Mr Miles,' she enun-
ciated with sarcastic clarity, 'I've been selling mews
houses for quite a number of years now, and I have
never—repeat, never—come across a potential pur-
chaser so utterly uninterested in what they were
being shown. You've been bored to sobs from the
moment we got here, so I assume that if you are
actually looking to buy this—or any other house, for
that matter—it's for somebody other than yourself.'

'Do you, Miss Radcliffe?' he countered midly,
gazing blandly into her flushed face.

'Yes, I do! In which case, may I advise that you
allow the lady in question to go around and view the
properties herself?' she told him heatedly, and
watched the blandness take on expression as his eyes
narrowed to study her for a long moment through
his lashes before he asked politely,

'And which lady in question might that be, Miss
Radcliffe?'

Julia stared back, a little glassy-eyed now, as she
realised what she had virtually accused him of. The
heated reference to 'the lady in question' had carried
the blatant insinuation that he was setting up a
mistress. She hadn't meant it to sound like that. Or
had she? Wasn't that exactly what she had thought
in her office—that he was looking for a house for his
girlfriend? Thinking was one thing, however, voicing
quite another. 'I apologise, Mr Miles,' she said stiffly.
'I had no right to make any assumptions.'

'No, you didn't,' he agreed lightly, 'although I
suppose a bit of fishing in the interests of gratifying
your feminine curiosity was too much to resist.'

'I was not fishing!' Julia flared up, infuriated all

over again that he was acting so contrarily and teasing—mocking her instead of putting her in her place as she had expected him to do. She could have dealt with a snub; being laughed at threw her. 'And it was not curiosity,' she denied in a belligerent mutter.

'Interest, then,' he amended carelessly.

Julia held his wry gaze stonily. 'Nothing about you interests me, Mr Miles,' she said with commendable frost which was at variance with everything else about her, then stood her ground as he came several steps closer when instinct warned her to move around to the other side of the kitchen counter—and quickly.

'I could change that, Julia,' he murmured with silky-soft menace, watching every nuance of her expression as she tried not to register any.

'I doubt it,' she tossed back with a lift of the chin, heard the deliberate challenge in the retort and wondered whether she'd gone barking mad. What was she doing, for heaven's sake? Throwing down the gauntlet?

His next step had her with her back against the kitchen counter, and it was as if someone had flicked a switch and suddenly increased the voltage in the charge of tension between them. The air was static with it—and with a strange, dangerous mix of excitement and threat that was unmistakably sexual. She had to do something and do it now—push him away. . .start talking—anything, before. . . She couldn't move; struck mute, she just kept staring into his eyes, her heart pounding in her ears as well as her chest.

The rational part of her mind refused to believe he would dare try to kiss her—or that she would let him; the irrational part must have done a complete flip, because she could already feel his mouth on her lips as he raised a hand to her chin and tilted her face up, examining it with the faintest quirk of a smile before lowering his head.

His mouth was so close Julia felt the warmth of his breath on her parted lips and, just possibly, might have closed her eyes in readiness for the kiss—she couldn't remember that bit, but the next instant sanity flooded back with the force of a bucket of cold water dashed over her. She swatted his hand away and was past him in one violent push, appalled that she had let him think, even for a moment, that she had wanted him to kiss her, and shaken that some crazy part of her had wanted him to so much.

CHAPTER TWO

'VIEWING's over, Mr Miles,' Julia rasped harshly, and didn't wait for him as she stormed across the room, down the stairs and out of the front door in a confusion of mortification and blind fury, but then she did have to wait until he followed her out— taking his time about it—before she could slam the door shut.

'I have another appointment just around the corner, so I won't trouble you for a lift back to your office,' Richard Miles said, as casually pleasant as if they had just completed a run-of-the-mill viewing, and whether he was tactfully lying or telling the truth was beside the point; Julia could have died of relief at being spared the anticipated nerve-racking drive closeted with him in the small car.

She forced herself to give him what she hoped passed for an expressionless glance. 'Fine, Mr Miles,' she said in a voice so strained it was remarkable it didn't crack.

'I rather thought it might be,' he murmured in a dry aside which Julia supposed she was meant to hear, and did. 'Thank you for your time, Miss Radcliffe.' The courteous afterthought was so formal, his expression so blandly innocent, that if it hadn't been for the faintly mocking light in his eyes Julia might have wondered if she hadn't imagined those crazy moments upstairs.

Had they really happened? In the safety of her car at last, she watched him stroll off down the mews, for all the world a perfectly ordinary, very handsome businessman, and, in the early spring sunshine bathing the pretty mews, so utterly unthreatening that it was preposterous that she had fled from him as if he had suddenly turned into a reincarnation of Jack the Ripper.

Julia tentatively touched her chin where his fingers seemed to have left a warm, tingling imprint. No way had she imagined *that*. Nor the strange tension or her own inexplicable, hostile attraction that might have culminated in lord only knew what if she hadn't come to her senses in the nick of time.

But—and it was a big, saving 'but'—she *had* come to her senses; she had *not* let him kiss her, she reminded herself grimly, and the next second was caught by surprise by the sharp, unexpected spasm of regret that came and went in a flash but not without leaving her shaken in its wake. Sorry that she hadn't let that arrogant macho male kiss her. . .? She must be in a worse state than she'd realised, and it was just as well she was leaving Dawlish today, because the way she felt she would have gone and ferreted Jeremy out of whichever restaurant and hurled her resignation at him right now.

It was all Dawlish's fault—every moment of the unsettling episode, she reasoned, unreasonably, because if it hadn't been for the last, nerve-fraying year taking its toll she wouldn't be like this. . .irrational and uptight, over-reacting to every word, every look, and being somehow vulnerable to the likes of Richard Miles, whom a year ago she would have taken in her stride and put in his place without losing her cool or her dignity.

Oh, forget Richard Miles, Julia ordered herself, exasperated, as she finally drove off. She would get back to the office, clear as many files as she could before five, abandon the rest and bolt out of the door—for good, which was what her sensible colleagues had done shortly after Charles Dawlish's sudden death.

Julia supposed it was shock and grief that had blinded her to the new reality longer than the others. Charles Dawlish had been her friend as well as the boss and mentor who had recognised her talent and burning ambition right from the start and set her career on its steadily upward path. Secretary to negotiator to senior negotiator, the next rung up the career ladder would have been to manager, and Mr Dawlish had even mentioned the possibility of partnership at a later date. And then he had died—at fifty-two, in a motorway pile up—and Jeremy Dawlish had materialised out of the blue.

One look at Jeremy, the unheard-of nephew and heir to the business, had sent one of the negotiators packing his bag two weeks later, and while her friend Andrew Reith had hung on for a few months, he too hadn't wasted much time. It was only Julia who had deluded herself into believing that everything would be all right once Jeremy found his business feet. Not even dear, soft-hearted Moira had harboured such idiotic notions, although the office administrator had also stayed, along with old Mr Matthews, the surveyor, out of simple loyalty perhaps. A year later, with the firm's formerly enviable reputation in shreds and Dawlish scraping for briefs, with new negotiators coming and going like tube station passengers, Julia too had finally thrown in the towel and resigned—without even a firm offer of a new job to go to. A rash move, but no more worrying than the damage she had been doing to her own career by having her name associated with Jeremy and Dawlish—not to mention the inevitable by-products. . .the blunting of her professional instincts, the gradual loss of motivation and initiative. . .the build-up of frustration and anger. Look at the way she had behaved this afternoon, for example. Julia preferred not to.

Suzie looked up from filing her nails as Julia came in, slamming the glass door behind her. She went over to Suzie's desk and thumped the keys down. 'Chiswell Mews,' she muttered, going through the motions of checking in the keys—a long-standing practice at Dawlish, but one which only she and Mr Matthews had bothered to follow in recent times.

Suzie glanced at them without missing a beat in her rhythmic filing. 'I think Julia's lost a sale, Miss Pagett,' she announced with a giggle to the plump, middle-aged woman emerging from the kitchen staffroom at the end of the office area with a cup of coffee in her hand.

'Oh, hello, Moira, you're back.' Julia managed a smile and made an attempt to rein in her bad temper.

'Ages ago, dear,' Moira told her cheerfully, 'but it was just my back luck to miss clapping my aged eyes on the devastatingly handsome Mr Miles, who Suzie tells me was nothing short of being the answer to every maiden's prayer,' the office administrator chuckled.

'Super!' sighed Suzie lavishly, and looked idiotic.

'Not this maiden's!' Julia retorted, heading towards her office—one of the half-dozen panel and glass boxes which lined a side wall and part of the back wall of the large room; with Jeremy and Deborah hardly ever in, the surveyor on holiday and two negotiators short, Dawlish might as well have rented out the offices for all the use they were put to these days. 'I take it some people have called it a day,' Julia observed witheringly with a pointed look at her watch which showed just gone three.

'They have,' confirmed Moira drily, following her into the office. 'However, your soon-to-be-ex-employer did telephone half an hour ago to tell me the monthly accounts session can wait until next month—so what else is new?—and, incidentally, to pass on his goodbye to you.'

'I'm touched to the bottom of my heart,' Julia returned sarcastically, too glad never to have to see Jeremy again to feel hurt any more by his cavalier attitude.

'Never mind, dear.' Moira's voice held suppressed anger. 'But whatever am I thinking of?' she exclaimed in the next breath, hurriedly putting her cup down on Julia's desk. 'You must be dying for a coffee. I'll bring you in a cup right away.'

'I'd love that—and a biscuit or three. I'm starving!' Julia called after Moira's disappearing back.

Not so starving that she was tempted by the remains of the sandwich curling up its edges in the drawer. Retrieving it from its impromptu hidey-hole, Julia secured it tightly in its paper bag and threw it into the waste-paper basket, then, proving old habits died hard, made a few jottings on the Chiswell Mews viewing—a follow-up procedure Mr Dawlish had always insisted on, and in this instance an exercise in non-committal brevity, finished by the time Moira returned with the coffee and what looked like the contents of an entire packet of shortbreads on a tray.

'This should keep you going until we have dinner.' Moira cast a disapproving eye at the files as Julia pushed them aside to make room for the tray. 'I wouldn't touch another one of those with a barge-pole if I were you; it's a waste of your time and you know it.'

Julia did know it, but it wouldn't stop her from tidying up as many as she could. Conscientiousness or plain masochism? She helped herself to a biscuit while Moira settled her plump body into the chair last occupied by Richard Miles and watched her approvingly for a moment or two like a mother hen.

'So what happened with Mr Miles to annoy you?' she asked when Julia had wolfed her first biscuit and picked up the second.

'Oh, I don't know. . .We just seemed to rub each other up the wrong way.' Julia played down the disconcerting meeting with a dismissive shrug. 'Started off on the wrong foot—that sort of thing,' she elaborated shortly in reply to Moira's questioning eyebrow, then felt uncomfortable under the steady scrutiny of the soft blue eyes across the desk. 'I didn't like the way he looked at me, if you must know.'

'How did he. . .look at you?'

'Oh, you know. . .' Julia muttered testily.

'Don't at all, I'm afraid.' Moira shook her greying head.

'Looked. Stared—too personally. You know,' Julia insisted in a sullen snap, glaring at Moira a little as enlightenment brought a broad smile to the office administrator's wrinkled face.

'Like a man looks at a very attractive young woman, I take it you mean. Not that I've much personal experience of it. Like to have had, though,' Moira added with an extravagantly wistful sigh that was such a perfect take-off of Suzie's that Julia would have laughed except that she was too annoyed.

'And he made a pass at me,' she blurted angrily, warmth gathering rapidly into her cheeks at the recollection of those last, strange tension-charged minutes and her own unaccountable reaction. To her surprise and chagrin, Moira laughed outright.

'Now don't scowl at me like that, Julia. Men do make passes at pretty girls. How else would the world continue to go around?'

'There's a time and place for everything,' Julia trotted out her own cliché with the primness of the caricature maiden aunt.

'True,' Moira conceded readily, 'and I admit Mr Miles should have exercised better judgement as to time and place, only I do sometimes wonder, Julia, whether there'll ever be a right time and place for you.' She wasn't smiling any more. 'Please don't jump down my throat, dear, but it does worry me that you won't make time for. . .well, socialising.'

'Men, you mean.'

'Yes, men.'

Moira had introduced conversations along these lines before. Julia didn't like them and Moira knew it. The older woman was a good friend, but that still didn't make it her business whether Julia chose to 'socialise' or not. Julia reached for a file—an officious hint which Moira couldn't, and didn't, miss. She stood up and started gathering up the cups, and instantly Julia felt mean.

'I know you mean well, Moira, it's just that I simply haven't got time for things like that. Anyway, I do go out with Andrew sometimes,' she added defensively. 'For drinks. . .a film.'

About to pick up the tray, Moira met her eyes in a long, steady look. 'Yes, you do,' she agreed flatly, and Julia flushed, knowing what Moira was thinking: that she only used Andrew and his silly infatuation with her when it suited her. Julia didn't much like that about herself, but she did want to go out sometimes, and Andrew was unthreatening, if a little irritating, and nearly always available.

Julia gave an abrupt, annoyed laugh. 'I won't even have time for Andrew when Weldons offer me that job on Monday. All right, *if* they offer me the job,' she corrected herself irritably as Moira frowned. 'And please don't remind me that I should have waited for a firm offer instead of resigning straight after the first interview.'

A tinge of pink swept into Moira's cheeks. 'What an old nag I must have turned into if you think I'm going to do that! I'm sure they'll offer you the job, darling, and that everything will turn out fine.' Just at the door, Moira turned around. 'What I'll never understand, though, is what it is that attracts you young people to those Dockland developments. First Andrew goes off to that big conglomerate that specialises in them, now you want to join the Weldons Dockland branch. They're all so slick and cut-throat and. . .' Moira tailed off, shaking her head.

'It's where the action is these days,' Julia pointed out for the umpteenth time, never really convincing her friend—nor herself, deep down. 'The commissions are colossal, and, if I want to set up my own agency in the next couple of years, then I've got to forget nice, genteel mews and mansion flats and go for the big time and the money—if they let me got a foot in the door,' she added in a mutter, meaning if Cliff Thomas, the manager of the Weldons Dockland branch, didn't see through her at the next interview and guess her real feelings about the Docklands, which were pretty much the same as Moira's. 'Don't worry, Moira, I've worked it all out; it's only an interim step—part of the overall plan.'

Moira sighed, unconvinced as ever. 'It's not. . ."you", Julia.'

'No, but where did being "me" get me this last year?' Julia countered bitterly.

'One week's orientation. . .finding your feet. Mr Weldon insists on that for everybody,' Cliff had told her after showing her around the office on the Monday following her second—successful—interview.

Spoon-feeding, Julia had thought, until she found out what 'finding your feet' actually entailed. . .coming to grips with advertising procedure. . .the selling-off plans, the ins and outs of property conversions, not to mention the 'familiarisation tours' of 'her properties'—a euphemism for being zapped around several enormous developments at a pace that left her breathless. Even at its busiest, Dawlish's pace had been horse-and-buggy by comparison.

She couldn't believe the pace at which the branch operated either, nor the number of negotiators, administrative and secretarial staff rushing about as if there were a deadline on each and every breath they took. Granted, the building also housed the head office of the large corporation, as well as the property development and commercial departments, but even without all those extra people the place would still have had the air of a sales week at Harrods.

Julia felt insignificant, overwhelmed, and dead on her feet at the end of each day, doubtful if she would see out the week, let alone the two years she had set herself. On the other hand, she had to admit there was something almost exhilarating about so much activity after the deadly flat months at Dawlish, and if she could just manage to adjust. . .fit in, and keep Cliff convinced that she was 'a natural' for the Docklands, she might last the distance yet.

She'd made it to Friday at any rate. Julia sat at her desk leafing through the list of properties which were to be advertised in the weekend papers—some of 'her properties' included—the ones she would be allowed to start selling the following week. There seemed to be a lot more people in the large, open-plan office than throughout the week, and a constant buzz of voices came from behind the elegantly simple screens, angled to partition off the negotiators' desks from one another. Her desk was at the front of the room, in a corner by the branch manager's office and the several other offices that anyone could use if privacy was needed.

An extra-loud laugh broke her concentration. Julia looked up, her glance not focused on anything in particular but chancing past some of the screens to the glass wall that separated the Docklands branch from the vast foyer, and that was when she saw him—Richard Miles, strolling into the foyer just as he had into her office at Dawlish, with that same air of owning the place.

Julia nearly took a fit, then, as she got over the nasty surprise, relaxed again, feeling quite safe behind her barrier of screens and glass wall as she stared at him.

He had come in with Cliff and a very attractive, dark woman who looked vaguely familiar. Julia watched curiously as the woman said something to Richard, smiled, then walked away towards the lifts. Someone on the staff, obviously—from Personnel most likely, because Julia was certain she had spoken to her recently, only she had met so many people in the last week, she could barely put names to half the faces yet. As she continued watching, Richard Miles and Cliff moved towards the entrance into the branch, and suddenly Julia's feeling of safety vanished as it dawned on her that they would need to virtually pass her desk on their way to Cliff's office.

The next moment was one of pure, childish panic. Leap up and run off to the loo? Hide in one of the empty offices behind her? Feeling an idiot, she remained at her desk. Perhaps he wouldn't recognise her. With her flaming red hair? Some hope, unless he'd been struck colour-blind in the last two weeks. But so what if he did see her? He was hardly going to demand what she was doing here or broadcast to all and sundry that he'd made a pass at her. Or that she'd been a hair's breadth from responding to it.

She couldn't see them behind the screens, but she could hear them coming closer. She snatched up a sheaf of papers off the desk and, head down, began flicking through them furiously, until in the end there was nothing for it but to stop the flurry of flicking and look up, because they had come around her screen and were there in front of her desk.

Oh, no, not me! Please don't foist him on me. Not for my first client, Julia mentally implored Cliff, focusing her glazed-eyed stare on him and not daring a glance at his companion.

'Julia, I think you've already met Richard. He's told me—— Oh, there's that call I've been expecting.' Cliff broke off the introduction as his telephone burst into peals in the office behind them. 'Excuse me, would you, Richard. . . Julia. . .?'

'Sure, Cliff,' Richard answered in cheery dismissal of the branch manager, quite amazing Julia that he was apparently so at home around the place, and that Cliff, too, felt so casual about this client he could walk off and leave him with her just like that.

With Cliff gone, she couldn't go on ignoring him. Her face rigid—the whole of her rigid—Julia turned to meet his eyes at last.

'Hello, Julia.' He used the husky purr that had the effect of physically brushing her skin.

She felt the familiar, annoying tingle shoot down her spine, but managed to hold his eyes steadily.

'Mr Miles,' she acknowledged him through her teeth, and then for one unnerving moment could feel his fingers under her chin. Involuntarily, her hand shot up to her face and came down again instantly, but not before she saw the amused flash in his eyes and knew she had given herself away. The surge of warmth into her cheeks only added the finishing touch to her mortification.

'How are you finding it at Weldons?' he asked chattily, drawing up a chair and sitting down, and anyone looking on might have assumed they were old friends. 'It must be quite a change for you after Dawlish.'

An understatement to end all understatements, only Julia had no intention of chatting to him about how she found her new job—nor anything else if she could help it. In growing anger, she eyed him leaning back in his chair with that same casual arrogance. . .the same air of taking control and giving her the same angry sense that he was playing games with her.

'Look, Mr Miles,' she began edgily, 'you probably think this is all terribly amusing—our coming across each other like this. I don't, and, although Mr Thomas had no way of knowing, you and I both realise that I'm not the negotiator you should be dealing with here at Weldons.'

'Aren't you?' he returned with fatuous innocence and a smile that was far too warm for comfort.

Julia's hand itched to check the buttons on her shirt. She was wearing the very same brown and cream outfit in this unwelcome replay of their first meeting, while he too had on his dark pin-stripe—

whether the same one or not, Julia couldn't tell. The pale, self-striped crisp shirt was different, though, and the tie a rich blue instead of maroon, silk, with a matching elegant flap of blue silk out of the breast pocket. All very businesslike and proper—if you took façade at face-value, and any woman who did that was asking for trouble. One 'viewing' with Mr Miles had been enough; Julia was not going to risk another.

'Mr Miles, you must feel as I do——' she began again, terribly reasonably, determined he was not going to provoke her into a display of unprofessionalism and get her fired at the end of her first week. 'Why don't you call me Richard, by the way? Everybody else around here does,' he cut in with his positively friendly suggestion.

Julia ignored the gratuitous invitation. 'Mr Miles, I think you'll agree that our initial meeting made it patently obvious that our personalities are not conducive to the conduct of any satisfactory business together, and——'

'Goodness, what a mouthful!' he interrupted her again, throwing his head back a little with the attractive laugh that rang around the room. 'What are you trying to say, Julia? Spell it out in plain English. Do I take it you don't want to take me around to view any more properties?' he prompted with a hugely amused grin when she didn't answer, and if Cliff happened to be watching through the glass upper half of his office wall he would think his new negotiator was getting along famously with his client—regular client, if everybody calling him 'Richard' was anything to go by.

'Precisely,' she snapped. 'But,' she went on

quickly, 'unlike at Dawlish, there are any number of negotiators here with whom you would feel more. . .comfortable, and who would be only too happy to take you around and help you decide on a property,' she told him, and heard herself sounding like a paid advertisement for Weldons' staff.

'But I feel very comfortable with you,' he purred back—predictably, and Julia had to clamp her teeth together for a few moments to prevent herself from snapping his head off.

'I'll explain to Mr Thomas that we. . .that I felt I didn't have the necessary experience yet to. . .to attend to your requirements,' she finished frostily as if he hadn't spoken, and could hardly believe it when he suddenly stood up.

'Heavens, I wouldn't want to put you through that sort of embarrassing confession to your manager!' he exclaimed with mock concern. 'Not when I know how important it is to you to stand on your dignity.'

He simply walked away, tossing a cheery wave in the direction of Cliff's office and leaving Julia furious at the parting shot and then very nervous and not knowing how she was going to explain the sudden walk-out to Cliff.

'Great chap, isn't he?' Cliff came bounding around the screen a few moments later. He bounded everywhere most of the time, Julia had noticed, and she had never met anyone so enthusiastic about everything. He was in his thirties, gangling-tall, fair and with an improbably young-looking round face, and Julia suspected Cliff was as sharp as a tack when it came to business—he had to be, to be manager of this particular branch of Weldons.

Her return smile was only brief that he hadn't asked why Richard Miles had left—which was a bit odd when she thought about it. 'Does. . .er. . . Richard drop in often?' she asked, puzzled by Cliff's attitude.

'When he can—which is not as often as he'd like to, unfortunately,' Cliff hastened to explain earnestly, not clearing up a thing as far as Julia was concerned. 'He always tries to keep in close touch with that's going on in the day-to-day side of the business. Doesn't he, Eleanor?' Cliff tossed the aside at Eleanor Bradley, Julia's immediate supervisor, as she joined them. 'Richard—likes to keep a weather eye on his staff, doesn't he?' Cliff clarified his aside as Eleanor raised an elegantly shaped eyebrow.

'Yes, he does,' Eleanor confirmed with a faint, curious smile at Julia. 'You'd met him before you joined us, hadn't you?' she asked, innocently, Julia supposed, but wasn't sure—of anything, as the gist of Cliff's enthusiastic wrap-up of Richard filtered through the stunned disbelief. 'His staff?' Richard Miles's staff. . .? Julia didn't want to believe it.

'Does. . . Richard. . .own Weldons?' she asked disjointedly. 'The whole lot of it, I mean,' she eleborated the naïve question hastily as they both stared at her strangely. 'All by himself? He hasn't a partner or. . .anything?' She elaborated some more, inanely, to cover up the awful fact that she hadn't known she had been talking—sparring—with her boss. . . Richard Weldon alias Richard Miles and a rotten, double-crossing trickster by any name.

Cliff's face cleared. 'Gosh, no, Richard owns every inch of Weldons—down to the last new branch. In

Kent, that one, and a great little branch,' he told her as proudly as if the latest addition to the Weldon empire had been a new baby in his own family.

Julia couldn't speak for fury, and then she met Eleanor's very curious dark blue gaze and rearranged her expression hurriedly. 'How. . .interesting,' she said fatuously.

'Great, eh?' Cliff was too wrapped up in his own admiration of his boss to notice her lack of any. 'Did Richard mention drinks to you?'

'Drinks?' repeated Julia blankly.

'Didn't you, Eleanor?' Cliff's voice held a tinge of accusation.

'I assumed Richard would when he said he wanted to have a word with Julia himself,' Eleanor replied crossly.

The discussion was going over Julia's head, and her face must have shown it.

'End of the first week of each month—if he's in, of course, which sometimes he isn't—Richard invites any new employees up to the boardroom along with their managers, to have a drink. All very informal. . .a welcome to the firm kind of thing,' Cliff informed her with the enthusiasm that right now was grating a lot on her nerves. 'Once in a blue moon there aren't any new employees, but in a place this size that's not often. There's usually someone most months, even if it's just a secretary or clerk. They get invited too,' Cliff added in a 'how about that?' voice.

'How. . .very egalitarian!'

Cliff missed the tartness; Eleanor didn't. The blue eyes stayed fixed on Julia's face, although Julia couldn't tell what was going on behind the carefully made-up façade—attractive in its thinnish, angular way, and it would have been more so if Eleanor hadn't favoured that particular shade of dark brown for her hair.

Cliff glanced at his watch. 'Four-thirty; time to pop up. You've told Tom?' he addressed Eleanor, referring to Tom Bennett, the other new negotiator who had commenced that week and whom Julia had barely seen about the place. Eleanor nodded. 'Right. There are a couple of chaps from Property Development I haven't met yet; should be a great group. All ready, then?' Cliff sounded as if he were mustering troops.

'You'll have to go up without me, I'm afraid,' Julia announced through a thin smile, having thought very fast while Cliff had been talking. 'I have a headache.'

Cliff's face fell absurdly. Eleanor didn't blink.

'What a bore for you! Perhaps you'd like to leave for home now,' she suggested unexpectedly. 'I can understand how this week must have been a great strain on you. New jobs always are, aren't they?' The question was rhetorical. Eleanor ran on smoothly. 'I'm sure Cliff won't mind your slipping away early, and you'll be able to have a good rest over the weekend since you're not expected in on the Saturday of your first week with us. You don't mind if Julia leaves now, do you, Cliff?' Her tone indicated the answer expected from him, and it was hard to say which of them was more surprised by this extraordinary show of concern—Cliff or Julia.

'Nooo. . . No, of course not,' the branch manager

rallied slowly with a nervous look at Julia as if he was afraid she was going to faint or take a fit.

'It's only a headache, for heaven's sake,' Julia repeated her lie testily. 'And I certainly don't need to go home,' she told Eleanor with a snap, furious with the woman for going out of her way to make such an issue out of what was patently an excuse to avoid going upstairs.

'Right,' Cliff said brightly, as if something very difficult had just been resolved. 'And why don't you get yourself a coffee. . .or something?' he suggested, edging away rather quickly.

'Yes, I'll do that,' Julia agreed, as anxious to see the back of them as Cliff was to get away. After they had gone she did go and make herself a coffee in the staff-room at the back of the reception area where a percolator was always on, and the coffee incredibly good—no expense spared, and it irked her that Richard Weldon thought highly enough of his staff to provide them with the best.

Now what? Julia asked herself, back at her desk with her coffee and still seething. Of all the unfair twists of fate—to land up with Richard Miles-Weldon for a boss! God, how he must have enjoyed leading her on! Damn it, she should have gone up to the boardroom and confronted him, then tossed in the job—she'd have to after that. She could still go up. . . Julia turned the idea over in her mind. But what would it achieve—aside from a couple of moments of gratifying satisfaction telling that devious man what she thought of his underhand business tactics in bowling into Dawlish under a false name to check her out, presumably after Cliff had discussed her after the first interview?

Everything was sickeningly clear now. . .his lack of interest in Chiswell Mews. . .the vague feeling she'd had from the start that he wasn't a bona fide client. . .that he was somehow baiting—testing, her. Which was what he *had* been doing, of course— setting her up to gauge how she handled clients who overstepped the mark. And how had she handled him? Over-reacted to his every word, every look. . .all but bitten his head off and generally behaved like a rank amateur. Worse than that, she had given the impression that she might even be receptive to the odd pass. Obvious now that his pass had been just another, particularly nasty, test. Pass or fail? Julia didn't know how to score herself on it, but did know she would never forgive him for it. Never.

Yet there was one thing that wasn't explained at all. Why, given her abysmal and utterly unprofessional performance, had Richard given the go-ahead for his branch manager to hire her?

'Headache better?' Eleanor asked tartly, materialising suddenly around the side of the screen and nearly making her jump.

Julia gave an abrupt shrug, suppressing the urge to tell Eleanor to put a sock in it. She studied her supervisor in silence, trying to figure out what was going on behind the pinched smile. . .why the veiled hostility—not just now, but always there from their first meeting. Eleanor didn't like her, fine; Julia didn't expect everybody to like her, but the senior woman's attitude carried an undercurrent of something more than just dislike. A resentment, Julia would have said, except she couldn't imagine why she should be singled out for some sort of feminine rivalry when there were already several other females within the branch, and Eleanor should have been used to working with women.

'Richard would like to see you up in the boardroom—if you're sure your headache is better—his words, not mine. I did explain that you felt unwell and that perhaps the stress of the job was getting to you,' Eleanor volunteered sweetly.

And made enough of a song and dance about the stupid white lie to give Richard and Cliff the impression they'd employed an invalid, thought Julia, really angered by the malicious misrepresentation.

'I shouldn't keep him waiting, if I were you,' Eleanor tossed over her shoulder as she left.

CHAPTER THREE

BOARDROOM: fourth floor, the in-house directory said. The lift decanted Julia into a thickly carpeted foyer where a middle-aged woman sat behind a reception desk in solitary and very silent splendour. As Julia approached, she looked up expectantly, a pleasant smile on her face which was rather homely, and a little reminiscent of Moira's, only this woman was a lot more elegant—to fit in with her surroundings, no doubt.

'I'm Julia Radcliffe. Mr Miles—I mean, Mr Weldon wanted to see me.'

'Yes, of course, Miss Radcliffe. Mr Weldon is expecting you.' The woman rose and led the way to one of several doors in the panelled wall behind her. She opened it without knocking. 'Miss Radcliffe,' she announced, and to Julia, 'Do go in.'

The door closed behind her. Julia took several steps forwards and looked down the long, rectangular room at Richard, standing at an enormous window that gave on to another building like their own, and past it, to the left, a glimpse of the top of the Tower of London. A quick flick of an eye told her she wasn't in the boardroom proper; there were armchairs and low tables dotted about—a place for more informal meetings. . .drinks. Some bottles and a number of glasses were in evidence on a sideboard by the wall, otherwise very little sign that a social gathering had taken place. One drink on the house and out, surmised Julia sourly.

Richard moved from the window, not in the familiar casual-arrogant stroll she had come to associate with him, but with a rigid tension in every stride that quite surprised her, because, caught up in her own fury, it hadn't occurred to her that Richard Weldon had anything to be furious about. He stopped by the sideboard and stayed there, studying her in a long, clamp-jawed stare in which he possibly counted to ten. 'Nice of you to decide to come,' he greeted her with a mirthless show of teeth.

So that was it: he was livid that she had ignored his invitation—order, rather—to the meet-the-boss drink session.

Coming up in the lift, Julia had decided to play it very cool, very casual, make out she had been terribly amused by his little deception—humour him, in fact, because she had reasoned that, in spite of her disliking the man thoroughly, it was in her own best interests to hang on to her job even if it meant doing herself out of the righteous pleasure of telling him what she thought of him and his tactics. The deadly smile, the sarcastic greeting, changed all that; Julia's good, sensible intentions went flying out of the window.

'Yes, isn't it?' she tossed the taunt at him with a fatuously arch smile, postponing just for a moment the barrage of angry words no job in the world was going to stop her hurling at him.

He wasn't expecting the jeer. Julia was pleased to note more tightening of the jawline. 'Don't ever try it

again, Miss Radcliffe,' he warned in restrained, thin-
lipped anger. 'When you're invited to drinks, you
come to drinks. I won't stand for lame——'

'Invited. . .?' Julia cut in with a strident laugh.
'Surely you mean "ordered", Mr Miles—oh, I forgot,
Weldon it is now, isn't it?'

Richard glared. 'My employees consider it an invitation,' he told her in a growl that nevertheless
seemed to have a defensive note in it.

'"Invitation" connotes choice, and your employees
wouldn't dare refuse to save their lives—jobs,
rather,' Julia retorted in heated scorn. 'Mr Miles—
oops, there I go again, I beg your pardon,' she
apologised sarcastically, 'Mr Weldon says "jump",
they say, "how high?", he says, "drink", they say,
"how many glasses, sir?" That's the way things are
around here, aren't they? Well, I've news for you,
Mr Weldon. This employee doesn't like things that
way and has no intention of jumping for you, high
or low, or drinking a drop on your orders. In fact,
she has ceased to be an employee of yours as of this
moment.' She lifted her wrist, flicked back her cuff
and made a great show of examining her watch. Five
twenty-five precisely. 'And furthermore, I would
never have demeaned myself to be an employee even
for a week had I known I was being employed by
you—or anybody else who'd stoop to such low-down
tactics as you used on me at Dawlish.' There, she
had done it—resigned in a fit of temper, and so much
for playing it cool. . .so much for needing the job.
She might regret it later, but for the moment the
sense of freedom to be able to say anything she
wanted to Richard Miles-Weldon, ex-client, ex-boss,

was positively exhilarating—if only she could think of something nasty enough while she was at it. 'I suppose you thought it all very funny,' she muttered, momentarily out of steam and dripping the sarcasm to make up for it.

'As a matter of fact, I did,' Richard admitted, his mouth relaxing from its thin, hard line and beginning to quirk infuriatingly at the corners, which was not the reaction Julia wanted.

'Yes, you would,' she shot back scathingly. 'Well, I thought it contemptible. And as for your charade this afternoon, it was pathetic. Childish.' The most cutting thing she could think of, and he didn't even appear to hear.

Head cocked slightly to one side, Richard contemplated her flushed, sullen face with a faintly pensive frown. 'You know what your trouble is, Julia?' he asked in the tone of voice of someone finally arriving at an illusive conclusion. 'You've got no sense of humour. Has anyone told you that? Oh, come on now, it was damned funny this afternoon.' He suddenly broke into a broad, boyish grin. 'If only you could have seen your face when Cliff brought me to your desk. The horror! It was all I could do to stop myself guffawing.' He chuckled in reminiscent enjoyment, while Julia stared through him, green eyes cold with disdain. 'And as for Dawlish. . .' Richard shrugged '. . .I'm not even sure what you're on about. I sprang you working at your desk with a sandwich, so what? It was lunchtime—everybody eats. You could have offered me half, I was starving. But no, you treated it as a capital offence to be caught eating. . .went all uptight and schoolmarmish and

determined to put me in my place like some delin-
quent schoolboy. What else could I do but needle
you a bit?'

Needle her a bit. . .? Oh, he had done that all
right—and more. He had embarrassed and infuriated
her. . .made a complete fool of her, and she was
supposed to take it all as a bit of harmless fun?

'Served you right when you couldn't get that car
out,' he added in a burst of almost childish spite,
then started laughing. 'Quite honestly, I thought you
were going to burst a blood-vessel.' Po-faced, and
definitely not sharing the joke, Julia watched his
laugh subside into a chuckle. 'See what I mean? No
sense of humour—uptight. . .dignity at all costs.'

'I fail to see any humour in your turning up under
an assumed name to spy on me,' Julia returned icily,
standing firmly on the dignity that he was making
fun of.

A heavy dark brow shot up. 'Back on our high
horse, are we? Frankly, I think I like you better hot-
headed. And anyway, it wasn't an assumed name,'
he went on, unperturbed by her accusation. 'My full
name is Richard Miles Weldon, and I just happened
to leave off one part of it for the occasion of our first
meeting.'

'Hah!' Julia pounced triumphantly as if he had just
proved her point. 'So I wouldn't know who you
were, which makes it exactly the same as using a
false name. And all that business about wanting to
view the house was pure time-wasting charade.'

'That's just your bad professional judgement,
influenced no doubt by your almost pathological

antagonism towards me. I was very interested in the house.'

'I don't believe you. It was just a ploy to. . .to see me in action,' Julia persisted, an edge of doubt creeping into her voice.

Richard lifted a dismissive shoulder. 'Simply a case of two birds with the one stone. I wanted to view the house *and* it gave me the opportunity to see you in action, as you put it.' He smiled drily. 'More easily achieved by leaving off the surname, sure, but hardly the sinister or contemptible deed you would have it. You'd have done the same in the same circumstances.'

It sounded vaguely plausible, yet he had barely given the house a second glance—a first glance, for that matter. Frowning, Julia watched him turn to the sideboard and pour himself a small drink. He looked across at her. 'Will you join me?'

Julia shook her head. 'No, thank you,' she refused politely, and wondered why she was still here—why she hadn't stormed out after hurling her resignation at him. . .why she was bothering to listen to his explanations. Curiosity, she supposed, and the feeling that there was more to be resolved between them—his pass: she wanted an apology from him for that, in which case she could be there all night.

Drink in hand, Richard turned to her again. 'I commenced negotiations for the house early this week; the matter is in the hands of my solicitor at this very moment.'

It had to be true, because he wouldn't lie about a thing so easily checked, was Julia's first thought; the second, that her so-called professional instincts hadn't been worth a bean.

'I shouldn't feel too badly about it, everybody loses a cinch of a sale once in a while,' Richard consoled her mockingly. 'But if it's any consolation, I'm not buying it for myself, so you were right about that part—and very perceptive of you it was too.'

'I don't need your pat on the head, thank you,' Julia snapped in knee-jerk response to the deliberate patronising, although she knew full well Richard was only baiting her. 'And if you hadn't carried on like a prize chauvinist, I would have been able to take your apparent interest in the house more. . .more professionally. You know exactly what I mean, so don't bother raising your eyebrows at me like that. I don't like silly macho games, Mr Weldon, or having passes made at me. Business tactics or no, it was out of line.' Just when she needed her dignity the most, her voice turned unexpectedly shaky. 'That part of your act was unjustified and unforgivable.' She managed to finish the tirade, but only in a sort of querulous whimper.

Richard held her eyes over the rim of his glass as he took a sip of his drink, then lowered the glass slowly and put it down on the sideboard. 'Act, Julia? What did you think was an act on my part?' he asked softly, his gaze unwavering. . .too intense, too— something that sent her rigid and on guard. Threatening.

She moved abruptly to the door. 'My resignation still holds, Mr Weldon. I don't want to work for you!' she flung over her shoulder, her hand stretched to the doorknob while she was still feet away, every instinct telling her not to stay around a moment longer.

'I don't accept your resignation, Julia,' Richard shot at her back crisply, without a shred of the soft warmth she had found so unnerving an instant ago, and, in spite of herself, she stopped and turned around and thought it was curious how Richard suddenly looked like his voice—crisply businesslike and faintly intimidating.

'Then I suggest you try harder, Mr Weldon,' she retorted with some of the tartness that had temporarily deserted her.

'You signed an agreement with Weldons,' Richard went on as if she hadn't spoken. 'Three months' trial period like all new employees in your position, and I expect you to honour it.'

A terms of employment agreement, not a contract; she could leave and they would hardly institute legal proceedings against her, but there had been an 'or else' in Richard's voice which intrigued as much as infuriated her, since he didn't have a thing he could threaten her with.

She took a couple of steps back into the room. 'Or else, Mr Weldon?'

'Or else, Miss Radcliffe, you might find it a little more difficult than you anticipated finding another agency to take you on.'

A sharp, stunned laugh burst out of her. 'You don't own every estate agency in London—yet!'

'No, but I own a considerable number of them and have contacts in a lot more,' Richard reminded her of the obvious, smoothly, and with malice.

Julia ranged her eyes over his impassive face. 'Are

you telling me you'd try to blackball me in the industry?' she demanded, genuinely amazed—not just by the implied threat, but by the ego of the man in believing he could; amazed, too, that he would even consider bothering to make things difficult for her just because. . . What. . .? She dared tell him a few home truths? That she dared throw his job in his face?

'Don't be so melodramatic, for heaven's sake,' Richard muttered testily. 'I'm merely suggesting that prospective employers might be curious as to why you couldn't hold down a job at Weldons for longer than a week.'

'That's not the way it sounded! And anyway, it's not a matter of "couldn't hold" but didn't want to,' Julia corrected him angrily.

'All the same, people would wonder, wouldn't they? And if you're thinking of not mentioning us, you might bear in mind that your appointment was listed in our trade rag just out. So come next issue and we'd have to put in that you'd left us. That would look odd, wouldn't it?'

Julia laughed gratingly. 'I'll manage to live with that, and, since there are enough agencies in this town which don't happen to think you're king of the castle in this business, I'll get by very well without your personal reference, thank you.'

'Ah, yes, there are the Dawlishes of the business.' The withering disparagement was a red rag to a bull. She and Moira might have deplored Dawlish's going to the dogs—they had every right to, no one else, least of all Richard Weldon.

The charge of indignation propelled her across the

room without a moment's thought. 'I'll have you know Dawlish was a very successful and very respected company—*is*,' she amended the tense belligerently. 'It's just going through a bad patch at the moment, nothing more.'

About six feet, Richard had an advantage of four inches or so—not much, but it made her have to glower up whereas he could look down—an unfair advantage, especially when he seemed more amused by her outrage than chastened. 'You win, I concede the point.' He threw up his hands in mock surrender. 'And whatever did it do to deserve such loyalty?' he added with a teasing smile.

'Mr Dawlish was very good to me,' muttered Julia, at a loss how to deal with this unexpected capitulation, at a loss how to deal with Richard Miles Weldon at all.

'Well, then, let's agree that Dawlish's loss is Weldons' gain, shall we, and no more talk about leaving?'

Julia ignored the fatuous gallantry and the attempt—blatant—to charm her out of her resignation. There was something she wanted to know, though. 'What I don't understand is why you hired me in the first place, given——' Given that she had given herself such a lousy reference, she meant, but couldn't quite bring herself to actually say it.

He shrugged lightly. 'Perhaps I just like very attractive, feisty redheads,' he drawled, baiting her; his eyes and smile told her that.

'That is a sexist comment!' Julia rose to the bait willy-nilly, mechanically lifting a hand to her warm cheek, then flicking back a strand of hair to give the hand something legitimate to do.

Richard laughed as if she had made a joke. 'If by that you mean I wouldn't say the same thing to a good-looking, short-tempered, redheaded chap, it is, I agree. But then I'm supposed to be—what was it? A prize chauvinist. . .?'

'Very droll.' Julia started moving back to the door in a hurry, not sure how she had come to be so far away from it. The side-lamp Richard had switched on earlier against the fall of darkness had changed the atmosphere of the room: it was cosier, more intimate, and it made Julia feel very uneasy. Vulnerable. It was one thing to have a business discussion—row—in office hours, but office hours had long passed and so, it seemed, had 'business'.

Richard reached the door before her and for one silly moment Julia thought it was to open the door for her.

'What are you running away from, Julia?' The low, husky purr was never more threatening, neither was the hard, lean masculine body blocking off her exit.

She was being fanciful. . .absurd. Of course Richard was not going to prevent her leaving. 'Don't be silly, Mr Weldon.' Julia tried to suppress the alarm from her voice by injecting an exasperated briskness into it, only she somehow ended up sounding curiously breathless and not at all like herself. As their eyes locked, she felt she was in a time-warp; she was back in the small sitting-room in Chiswell Mews, the tension between them palpable and heightening, and her heart thumping so loudly Richard must have heard. An anticipatory little shiver shot through her.

She knew he was going to kiss her and knew that, however insane it was, she was going to let him. Just this once. Just this once she wanted—needed—to know. . .to feel what it was like to be kissed by those faintly mocking lips. Madness. Julia gave a little shake of the head—a token 'no', to herself as much as to Richard.

'I think you mean yes,' he contradicted softly, curving a hand under her jaw to cup it firmly as he brought his mouth to her lips, parting them and taking possession of her mouth as if it had always belonged to him.

The first moment of contact was like going into shock, or suspended animation perhaps. . .not breathing, not thinking, not even feeling, and then when sensation returned it was to a warm, throbbing consciousness of the kiss deepening very slowly and with an inexorable voluptuousness that melted every bone and muscle in her body.

Julia's response was a mindless surrender to the sweetly overpowering mouth. In a haze of almost languid sensuousness she kissed him back, answering depth with a depth and a voluptuousness all her own, that later she found shocking—a part of herself that was a complete stranger to her. When Richard finally broke off the kiss it was too abruptly and too soon. She felt disorientated—as if she'd come suddenly out of warm fuzzy darkness into a blaze of light.

'I think we've just kissed and made up, don't you?' Richard sounded, and looked, so casually cheerful, it threw her back into momentary disorientation again.

'What's the matter, Julia?' His eyes were faintly puzzled by whatever it was showing in her face.

What was the matter? Julia nearly laughed. She had never been kissed like that in her life, nor ever kissed a man like that. She felt as if the ground had given way under her feet, and he was as unaffected as if they had just shaken hands. What *had* she expected? A tremulous declaration that she'd turned his world upside-down? Hardly. Yet the naïve adolescent in her must have expected something—what, Julia had no idea, and would have died any number of ghastly deaths before letting slip the smallest hint that she wasn't the woman of the world he so obviously took her for. Sophisticated adults probably kissed like that for practice.

She had dropped her eyes for fear of what they might betray, and tried to put on a nonchalant show of adjusting her cuffs. 'I really must go,' she heard herself saying, quite gaily.

'Julia. . .' The tone of voice made her glance up. It held a curious, uncharacteristic uncertainty she had never heard in it before. 'Come and have dinner with me,' Richard said, and there was nothing uncertain about the invitation; it was casual, seemingly spur-of-the-moment, and three hours later he would probably follow it up with a 'come to bed with me' because she had virtually given him the come-on.

'I've resigned, Mr Weldon, remember? You can't order me to dinner—or anywhere else,' she pointed out nastily, all her hostility back from wherever, and making her feel the safer for it. Richard had moved slightly from the door—enough for her to reach out and fling it open, which was as far as she got.

'Now, just a minute!' He grabbed her arm to prevent her dash from the room. 'I did not order you to dinner, I invited you,' he rasped, a surge of angry colour in his cheeks. 'What's got into you, Julia? One minute you give me to understand that——'

'That I'm available?' she finished for him acidly.

'That you're. . .what?' Richard looked as if he didn't know whether to laugh or shake her; the grating sound and tightening of his grip was possibly a compromise. 'Come off it, Julia, it was just a kiss, for heaven's sake. You wanted it as much as I did, *and* enjoyed it just as much,' he reminded her with a spurt of malice.

She couldn't deny something that had been so humiliatingly obvious, and the 'it was just a kiss, for heaven's sake' was really spelling it out for her. Her face felt on fire as she stared helplessly at him.

'What are you running away from, Julia?' The same question he had taunted her with earlier.

You. Me. . . The feeling of being threatened by something she didn't understand—whatever the answer was, Julia wasn't going to try to work it out right now. 'I'm not running away from anything,' she lied shakily. 'I'm in a hurry because I'm late for my date.' The second lie was desperate inspiration, but she would have resorted to her grandmother's funeral to get out of the room and away from him.

'Date?' Richard repeated as if he had never heard the word before.

'Yes, date,' Julia confirmed quickly, and this time the lie served its purpose; he released her abruptly.

'Goodnight, Mr Weldon,' she muttered, and in her haste to get out of the room nearly walked into Cliff, who had bounded silently across the thick carpet of the reception area.

'Hello, Julia, still here?' Cliff beamed, no doubt making a mental note of her dedication in staying so late—after that terrible headache too.

'Julia has a date,' Richard announced sarcastically behind her. 'We mustn't keep her any longer.'

'Great,' said Cliff, sounding really pleased for her.

'Isn't it?' Julia muttered, making her escape at long last, and was halfway home, having skirted the City and as much of the bustling West End as she could, when it dawned on her that in her fury and agitation she'd driven off in the company car—a small Peugeot like her previous one, but this one owned by Richard Weldon.

You handed in the car keys and caught a bus home when you stormed out of a job. Monday, Julia promised herself. Monday she would return to hand the keys in to Cliff and tell him she had decided Weldons wasn't her scene. And Richard Weldon could tell him whatever he liked, only Julia was quite sure he wouldn't be spreading it about that she had left because she didn't want to work for him, and, contrary to whatever irrational signals she might have unwittingly sent out, did not like passes made at her and had no intention of staying around for more. Or for being lined up for one of those routine office flings which was what she suspected he had had in mind.

Perhaps some women might have jumped at the chance; after all, there was nothing like an affair with the boss for getting ahead—for the duration of the affair at least, after which, it was out of the door and looking for a new job according to the age-old pattern of office romances, while the boss trotted back to the wife or girlfriend in the wings—in the mews house, more like—until another ninny turned up for the next fling. No way was Julia ever going to be part of that kind of no-win scene; she was out of the door by choice, and if that was 'running away' then more speed to her running shoes.

She turned into the short mews where she lived, a stone's throw from Kensington High Street—and just another throw from Chiswell Mews. Was he really buying that house? And for whom? 'And who cares?' Julia muttered aloud. Richard Weldon could buy up every house in the whole mews for all she cared. *And* install a girlfriend in each of them.

She garaged the car and went upstairs, doing a mental check of the contents of the refrigerator to work out if there was anything she could concoct into a meal, and half wishing there really had been a date. . .that she'd accepted Andrew's invitation to dinner to celebrate getting the job at Weldons—only in this case it would have been to celebrate her resignation! Julia had put him off, saying she would probably be too tired, and suggested leaving it for a couple of weeks until she was ready to come up for air again. The real reason was that she had decided to try and stop using Andrew as a prop whenever she felt down or needed company; it simply wasn't fair on him when he persisted in thinking of her as his girlfriend, while she would never be able to see him in terms of 'boyfriend'.

She didn't want or need a boyfriend—not Andrew, not anybody. Yes, once in a while she might wish she had a relationship of some sort, and in her fleeting fantasies the man waiting for her at the end of a hard day was a fuzzy, comfortable figure in tweeds and cords and glasses—the very antithesis of the debonair, sophisticated father she couldn't remember. Or to Richard Weldon. A Charles Dawlish type, reliable and unthreatening, and sometimes Julia had to wonder whether the mythical man wasn't a surrogate father figure. Whatever he was, there was no room for even him in her life right now, and unless she got herself a cat there wouldn't be anyone to come home to for a long while yet—not until she was firmly established in her own agency and completely independent. *That* was what she had to keep her energies for.

Single-minded, Moira had called her—a tactful euphemism for 'obsessive', Julia suspected, and resented it, because if she was it was only that she couldn't afford not to be.

She had learnt the hard way what it meant when a woman didn't have the means to be independent. . .learnt it first-hand after her father had deserted her mother before Julia was two, not even a child managing to tie him to the woman who had forced him into one of those anachronistic 'shotgun marriages'. Later, when she was older, she had learnt everything there was to know about money worries, about soul-destroying, dead-end jobs her mother had had to take because she hadn't been trained for anything better. If nothing else, Elise Radcliffe had passed on to Julia a deep, bitter distrust of men and their motives, and instilled into her daughter a burning determination to make it on her own.

And she was a considerable way towards it already, thanks to her mother's obsessive saving in the years before she died of the cancer Julia always believed was stress-induced. That was six years ago, and at nineteen Julia had been left the deposit towards a place of her own—her mother's express wish. She had bought a run-down bedsit, renovated it and sold it astutely, then did the same with the next property, a tiny, one-bedroomed flat, the sale of which had netted her the sizeable deposit on the small mews house she now had. Charles Dawlish's guidance had been invaluable in every transaction, as it had been in setting her on a career path. How different things would be if he were still alive; she'd be managing Dawlish now, and not out in an alien environment like the Docklands trying to make the proverbial fast buck.

Only she had just stormed out of Weldons and the pots of commissions she had been banking on, and talk about cutting off your nose to spite your face. Or had she? There were other agencies specialising in Dockland properties—like the one Andrew was working for, for starters.

Leaving her omelette unfinished, Julia jumped up and ran to the telephone. That was it. She would ring Andrew and ask him if he could try to get her into Fenwick and Jeffcott. True, it would be a bit embarassing confessing she had left Weldons after just one week, but she'd think of something.

'Julia, hello! Changed your mind about dinner tonight, have you?' Andrew's instant leap to the wrong conclusion about the reason for her call put Julia momentarily off her stride.

'What dinner? Oh, no. No, sorry, Andrew,' she remembered, and recovered herself quickly. 'It's been a long, hard week and I really do need an early night.'

'I'm not surprised,' he returned with a sympathetic laugh. 'Takes some getting used to after Dawlish, doesn't it? I didn't know what hit me when I came to Fenwick's, and it'd be worse for you, of course.'

'Worse for me? Why?' Julia asked sharply, frowning as the pause lengthened at Andrew's end. 'What did you mean, worse for me?' she persisted more sharply.

'Nothing much, Julia, honestly,' Andrew muttered reluctantly, as if he was wary of putting his foot in it, and she could picture his thin, mobile face working through its funny range of nervy expressions when he had to think in a hurry. 'Only that it would be so different for you—selling in the Docklands, and at Weldons, of all places.'

'They're not any different from the place you're with now—nor the places you're selling, for that matter,' Julia pointed out snappishly.

'No,' he agreed hastily, 'but—well, it's just hard to imagine you in with that lot when you—well, you know. . .'

Julia knew; when you used to jump on your soapbox and rant about artificial environments. . . speculators, big, impersonal estate agency conglomerates—and cite Weldons as your prime example! Andrew was too tactful to actually say all that, but that was what he meant.

'It's a woman's prerogative to change her mind,

haven't you heard?' Julia tried for facetiousness and sounded waspish.

'Sure.' Andrew gave an edgy laugh. 'So you're managing OK, then?'

'Great,' she lied, piqued by the faint insinuation that she wouldn't be able to manage. 'I've only just finished the first week, of course, but I'm already loving it,' she trilled, and, damn it, how could she ask him about jobs after that?

'That's terrific,' Andrew said ultra-heartily. 'Sure you don't want to come out tonight so you can tell me all about it?'

'No, Andrew, really I——'

'What about tomorrow night, then?'

Would he never give up? Julia suppressed a groan. 'I half had in mind to go down to Kent for the weekend—you know, my cousin Derek's place,' she fibbed, a little lamely, and thought what a liar she was turning into of late.

'Oh. Well, it will have to be lunch next week then, won't it?'

'I could be rather busy next week.' That at least was true—she'd be flat out job-hunting. 'But I'll give you a ring and let you know how things stand.' She hung up as quickly as she could after that, and could have kicked herself for the botch she had made of the call. Why hadn't she told Andrew straight off that she had walked out of Weldons and needed a new job, but fast? Pride? Because Andrew would have immediately assumed she hadn't been able to handle the pace? Wasn't that what Richard had warned her people would think? Oh, lord, what was she going to do now?

Eat humble pie and stay at Weldons, she had decided by the end of the awful, depressing weekend. If she had felt too uptight and embarrassed to ask even Andrew about jobs, what hope did she have of getting herself through a new set of interviews? None.

CHAPTER FOUR

JULIA left the Peugeot in the multi-storey car park where Weldons had an entire floor reserved for its staff, and was hurrying towards the office when the footsteps a short distance behind her seemed to quicken. She spun around, and then didn't know what to do when she saw it was Richard.

It was just after eight, and she had come in early especially to go and wait for him in his suite to tell him she had reconsidered her position over the weekend and wanted to withdraw her resignation. All the way in from home she had rehearsed her lines, bracing herself for the humiliating encounter, yet now that it had come upon her a little sooner than anticipated she felt unnerved. She dithered, and he caught up with her.

'Good morning.' The man who had kissed her on Friday night greeted her on this Monday morning with the casualness he might have greeted his cleaning lady; the voice was just as casually pleasant, and to Julia the impersonal politeness was more discouraging than if he had snarled at her.

'Good morning,' she returned tightly after a disconcerted pause, and fell into step with his stride, careful to keep distance between them and urging herself to get on with it. Every silent step was only making her more nervous. 'I was hoping to see you before the others came in,' she plunged in at last as their office block loomed into sight.

'Were you?' Richard enquired with the same daunting politeness.

Julia flicked him an apprehensive glance and, when he continued looking ahead with no attempt to prompt, she blurted in a rush, 'I've reconsidered my resignation and would like to withdraw it—if that's all right with you,' she put in hastily, tossing another nervous look at him, and, as he turned to meet her gaze, she could have sworn there was amusement lurking behind the screen of dark lashes.

Damn it, he was loving every moment of her discomfort! Julia's humble employee act suddenly wavered precariously, but only for an instant. She wanted the job, didn't she, and starting off another round of hostilities with the boss was not on her new agenda.

The automatic doors of their building slid open. Richard motioned her to precede him inside, and then just inside the foyer he said, with po-faced solemnity, 'Very well, Miss Radcliffe, you may retain your job. On one condition.'

'Condition?' She threw him a startled frown.

'That you have dinner with me tonight.'

Julia stopped dead in her tracks. 'That's not fair!' she yelped in indignation.

Richard lifted a nonchalant shoulder. 'I only play fair when it suits me, Miss Radcliffe. I'll pick you up at your place at eight—and no, don't bother giving me your address, I'll find it in your file,' he added, with fatuous helpfulness and a maddening smile.

As if she had any such intention! About to tell him

what he could do with his dinner, she became aware that Eleanor had just come in, and, since they were blocking her way, was sort of politely hovering behind them. Thwarted out of her tirade, Julia flung a last, murderous look at Richard and marched off without another word towards the branch entrance, and what Eleanor would make of her bad-tempered exit Julia could not have cared less.

She could—would—refuse to go. . .simply not be at home, and there was not a thing Richard could do about it; you couldn't impose outrageous conditions like that, nor sack someone because they refused to go out with you—certainly not in this day and age of sexual discrimination laws which she would quote to him chapter and verse—and enjoy it.

On the other hand, if she did *choose* to go. . . Julia mulled over that alternative when her temper had subsided, and by the end of the day had reasoned herself out of a boycott of the dinner. A few hours in a neutral environment might provide an opportunity to set things straight between them. . .establish, belatedly, a detached businesslike relationship, and if she planned on staying at Weldons for the next couple of years then, the sooner they did that, the better. That had been the gist of her weekend of rationalisation—the new agenda she had come up with. . .being businesslike, distantly polite and staying cool at all costs.

Cool? She nearly jumped out of her skin when the buzzer sounded downstairs that evening, and then she went flying to the bedroom mirror to check, yet again, that the simple cream wool dress still looked as good as when she had put it on half an hour earlier. The idiotic attack of adolescent panic would have been funny if it hadn't been so pathetic to be acting like a teenager faced with her very first date. Richard was not a date and she was twenty-five, not fifteen, although Julia suspected the average fifteen-year-old would have left her for dead when it came to composure and experience of men.

The clock on the small church in the nearby square was striking eight as she opened the front door. 'Hello, how very punctual.' Her nerves had her trilling so graciously she was practically cooing.

'I believe it signifies underlying insecurity,' Richard grinned, and brought an involuntary snort of a laugh out of her. If Richard, super-confidence personified, had any insecurities, then it would take a dozen psychologists a lifetime apiece to unearth them. 'You look very nice,' he went on after the miss-nothing once-over that made her wish she were still in her office outfit. Now he would think she had put herself out to look nice for him, and that was not the impression she intended to convey. 'I'm sorry I haven't had time to go home and change; Cliff wanted something sorted out at the last minute, and it took ages,' Richard apologised—unnecessarily, considering he looked his usual crisply handsome self, and it was a fair bet he knew it, thought Julia tartly as she slammed the door closed behind herself. When Richard reached to take her arm, she swung out of his range so pointedly she might as well have jumped three feet in the air and yelled 'don't touch me!' She felt as embarrassed as if she had, and so much for staying cool.

Richard ignored the over-reaction. 'I left the car

around the corner because I thought we'd just walk to one of the bistros in the main street. What do you think?'

'Fine,' she agreed with an indifferent shrug, and set off down the mews with an angry clatter of high heels over the uneven cobblestones.

'You're really mad at me, aren't you?' Richard muttered, piqued, when they got to the arch at the end of the mews without exchanging a word.

'Good gracious, why should I be?' Julia returned in heavy-handed mock surprise, and pulled her arm hurriedly into herself because Richard's arm was almost brushing against it.

He made a sound of exasperation under his breath. 'For Pete's sake, stop acting as if I'm about to attack you! Every time I come within a foot of you, you just about take off.'

'Don't be ridiculous,' Julia snapped, grateful that the furious heat in her cheeks wouldn't show under the street lights.

'See?' Richard took her elbow in a firm grip to walk them across the road. 'Like an ironing-board.'

'I don't like——' she started belligerently, and cut herself off abruptly.

'What?'

'Nothing.'

'Being touched? Is that what you were about to say?' Richard released her immediately they reached the other side of the road. 'You can relax, Julia, I promise I won't make anything remotely resembling a pass. . .'

The sentence wasn't finished. Julia flung him a

suspicious, expectant glance and waited for the punchline.

'Until you indicate that you want me to again,' he finished matter-of-factly, and made her give a shocked little indrawn gasp at the presumption.

What did he think he was—irresistible? She might have temporarily—inexplicably—taken leave of her senses once, but that once had been more than enough.

'Don't hold your breath!' she said shakily.

'I won't. This do?' Richard veered suddenly into the first of the bistros which made up an extensive stretch of pleasant eateries just before the main shopping area.

'It's your party,' Julia muttered back sullenly.

It was an Italian-type bistro, already full with early diners and noisy with chatter and laughter. A wise choice of venue, Julia had to concede. . .very casual, very public. Very unthreatening. She hadn't really expected him to spring candle-light and soft music on her, but with Richard Weldon it was best not to assume anything.

The bright-eyed young man, white teeth flashing under an extravagantly black moustache, settled them at a table, handed them a menu each and swirled off like a ballet dancer.

Julia glanced around.

'All right?' Richard asked, solicitously like an anxious-to-please date.

Julia gave a small nod. 'Yes,' she said shortly, since there was nothing at all wrong with the place, only with her being there with Richard. 'Don't you think it's time you got to the point and told me what this dinner is all about?'

'What's the point of any two people going out to dinner? To talk. . .get to know each other better, not least to eat. Speaking of which, why don't you decide what you want to order?' He deflected her question with no attempt at subtlety and gave his attention to his menu.

Why not? thought Julia, and lowered her eyes to her own menu. Food had been the last thing on her mind that day, and, with the weekend meals scratched up out of bits and pieces, it seemed forever ago that she had last eaten properly; whatever Richard's ulterior motive in forcing her here, the by-product was at least a decent meal and she might as well enjoy it.

She ordered a seafood crêpe to start and a veal dish to follow, and then they talked, a little stiltedly, of neutral things like restaurants and favourite cuisines until their food arrived, and then Julia was very conscious of other people's chatter and laughter whirling around them as they concentrated on their respective dishes in a silence that seemed to isolate them from the rest of the diners. From each other too, and if the aim of the exercise was to 'get to know each other better' then all they had achieved so far was knowing they both liked French and Italian cuisine.

'What about pudding?' Richard suggested when the waiter came to remove the plates from the main course.

'Just coffee, please.'

He gave the order for two coffees. 'So how have

you settled in at Weldons?' he asked, returning his attention to her, and catching her off guard with the introduction of 'business'.

'OK. I think,' Julia qualified unthinkingly, and then wished she hadn't because it had made her sound so doubtful.

'Cliff tells me you learn fast, are a self-starter and keen as mustard.'

'He does?'

'You sound surprised.' Richard was watching her intently.

'I'm flattered,' Julia corrected with an embarrassed laugh. 'I mean, it's another world and I didn't really think I'd——' Fit in, she nearly said before stopping herself in the nick of time, suddenly wary and very aware that she was talking to her boss and, if she wasn't careful, she could let slip that she wasn't nearly as keen on her new environment as Cliff thought her. 'It's very exciting,' she hurried on, quite gushing, 'and I can hardly wait to be let loose— actually start showing people around and getting my teeth into some real negotiating.' Was she overdoing the enthusiasm? This was not an interview; Richard was not out to trap her into betraying how she really felt about big, fast-paced agencies like Weldons Dockland branch, and Dockland developments themselves. Or was he? 'I found I was getting terribly jaded in the mewsy set-up,' Julia couldn't stop the babbling. 'Dreadfully stale. . .'

'Were you?' Richard prompted with no particular expression.

'Oh, yes. Even before Mr Dawlish died I was thinking of leaving to spread my wings,' she went on lying barefacedly while she crossed her fingers on her lap in childish insurance against a bolt of lightning.

'Into the Dockland developments?'

Was there a note of scepticism in his voice? 'Well, that's where the action is these days, isn't it? The money, anyway,' she retorted rashly, and tinkled out a hasty laugh as if she had made a joke. 'What about you?' She changed tack in a hurry when Richard didn't laugh. 'Do you enjoy being in real estate?'

'It's very exciting,' he said, po-faced, and made her flare red at how fatuous she must have sounded when she had said that.

Later, Julia couldn't work out what the end of the evening, or any other part of it, had been all about. Richard had talked mainly business, drawing her out about her early years with Dawlish, eliciting her opinions on various aspects of the London property market. . .and in a way Julia had felt more threatened than if he had been launching an all-out campaign to charm her into bed, when he hadn't so much as come within sneezing distance of hinting it. He walked her home quite early, said the conventional 'goodnight and thank you for a pleasant evening,' and left without even an attempt at a peck on the cheek, and, when next they met at the office, was the epitome of the pleasant, polite, unthreatening boss.

And that was the way it continued during the following busy weeks. Even when they happened to find themselves alone, like walking to the office from the car park, Richard chatted about work, the weather, a television programme, exactly as Cliff might have done, or any of the negotiators. Once he had asked, teasingly, if her allocated car space was adequate for her needs, and Julia had laughed and wondered whether she was beginning to like him.

'What about having lunch with me today?' he suggested lightly about three and a half weeks after the curious dinner. They had arrived at the car park together that morning—a coincidence which occurred several times a week.

Julia's first reaction to the unexpected invitation was as unexpected as the invitation itself: a little spasm of surprised pleasure, and the 'yes, I'd love to,' was on the tip of her tongue when she remembered that today was the day of the long-deferred lunch with Andrew, whom she had already put off twice, and finally she had run out of excuses.

'I'm afraid I can't today,' she told Richard with genuine regret. 'I'm lunching with a friend—an old friend. Girl-friend,' she fibbed—pathetically, she thought later.

'Too bad. Another day, perhaps.' Richard sounded if he could not have cared less, which stung her into wishing she had said she was lunching with her boyfriend.

And what would that have achieved? Needled Richard into showing jealousy? A daft—and dangerous—way of giving her ego a boost when experience had made it only too plain that she could not handle anything vaguely 'personal' between them. Richard had got the message and backed off, and she should have been relieved and grateful, and not tempted to rock the tentative new status quo which had developed over the last few weeks.

It was grey and drizzling when Andrew picked her up outside Weldons. Dark and always wiry, he looked thinner than ever even with the heavy navy mac on, and still radiating that nervy energy Moira used to call plain hyperactivity. Julia was warily pleased to see him. In his last telephone call he had insisted he had something to tell her which would really floor her, and Julia very much hoped it would be an announcement of his engagement; far from being floored, she would have been relieved first, and then truly delighted for him.

'Wait until you hear what I've got to tell you!' he announced in suppressed excitement after greeting her with a quick peck on the cheek, then all along the short drive to the pub he was like a small boy with a secret—dying to spill it but reluctant to part with it until he'd dragged out the maximum of frustrated curiosity from his audience.

'I'm still waiting,' Julia told him laughingly when he brought their drinks to the table; mineral water for her, a small beer for himself.

Andrew grinned as he squashed himself into the scrap of space beside her on the padded bench that lined the pub's wall. The place was full and they had queued the best part of fifteen minutes at the counter for their meal. A very popular Docklands pub, and much frequented by Andrew and his new colleagues, it seemed, with Andrew flapping a wave at practically half the people there.

'Have you spoken to Moira recently?' he asked— another fob-off, it sounded to Julia. She checked her irritation.

'Not recently, no,' she confessed with a nudge of

guilt. 'I meant to give her a call the other week, but. . .' she shrugged '. . .there just hasn't been the time.' Nor the need, she could have added, since resolving her differences with Richard and settling into Weldons. 'The last time I spoke to her was when she rang me in my first week with Weldons to see how I was getting on. Why?'

'She mightn't know anything about it yet either,' Andrew said cryptically. 'I only picked it up by chance myself and——'

'Andrew, what on earth are you talking about?' Julia burst out, her patience at an end. Obviously his secret was not a sudden engagement, but she was not prepared for the final divulgement.

'Weldons buying up Dawlish.' He watched her face avidly, and the effect of his news on her tickled him hugely. He gave a hoot of satisfied laughter. 'Thought that would give you a jolt! You hadn't heard? I did think you might have got wind of it—working for him and all that. How's it going, by the way? Still loving it?'

'Yes,' Julia returned mechanically. 'When? When did Richard Weldon buy Dawlish?' she demanded, not sure she really believed it.

Andrew pursed his lips and gave a shake of the head. 'Can't say. In fact, I'm not sure the deal is even completed yet,' he admitted reluctantly. 'Probably going through right now, although it's my bet he approached Jeremy—or vice versa—weeks ago. About the time you left, I shouldn't wonder. Pity about that, isn't it—you leaving when you did? You would have been first in line for branch manager for sure, if you'd hung on, in spite of that ass Jeremy doing his darnedest to ruin the business as fast as he could.'

That was the gist of the whirling thoughts in Julia's dazed mind. If only she had hung on. . . If only she'd had an inkling that Jeremy was planning to offload the business. If only she hadn't reached the end of her tether for another couple of weeks.

'Never mind, just bad luck,' Andrew consoled her with trite sympathy, then took an enormous mouthful of his steak and kidney pie and stayed mercifully silent while he concentrated on the business of chewing.

Julia couldn't touch her quiche. Sick with disappointment, she stared glumly across at the bar until she realised the young chap behind it was winking at her. She scowled and turned away.

'You could still apply for it, you know—the managership,' Andrew was suggesting helpfully. 'Unless, of course, he's already got someone lined up for it. Have you met him, by the way? Richard Weldon? Of course, you would have,' he answered himself when Julia didn't, 'he'd be around the place a lot, and anyway, he's always in on the second interview, isn't he, so you'd have met him then?'

Julia was too distracted to ask how he would know about Weldons' second interviews. . .too caught up in her own anger with Richard for not mentioning anything to her when he must have known how interested she would be. And then it was lucky she wasn't chewing on anything, because she would have choked with the next thought. That dinner! Had Richard intended to sound her out about the managership that evening? Oh God, what a mess she had made of trying to be clever. . .rabbiting on like a twit about outgrowing Dawlish. . .mews—becoming jaded, for heaven's sake, when she'd have given her eye-teeth and a whole lot more for a chance to run dear old Dawlish properly. Altogether, she could not have put her foot in it more if she'd tried—if she had sat and thought for a week of the best way to sabotage her own career. But, damn it, Richard should still have mentioned it to her. He had had any number of opportunities during their strolls from car park to office, and she could have tried to explain, somehow, how she really felt about Dawlish and mews, and that she wasn't the hyped-up Docklands agent she was trying to make herself out to be.

The drizzle had urged itself into a consistent rain and was quite heavy when Andrew pulled up a little way down the block from Weldons, and unusually, for Andrew, had the good sense not to try to badger her into another lunch or dinner, or anything else. Julia had not brought her umbrella with her, so he chivalrously insisted on walking her back to the office entrance under the shelter of his big black brolly.

'Cheer up, Julia, do!' Holding the brolly high above their heads with one hand, Andrew suddenly tilted her chin up with the other and gave her a kiss. . .a cheering-up-a-friend kiss, nothing more, but who was to know what sort of kiss it was if all they could see was what for all the world looked like a romantic couple parting lovingly under an umbrella in the rain? Not Richard, as he drew alongside them just as Andrew was taking his hand away from her chin.

Richard gave them a curt nod. 'Miss Radcliffe,' he

acknowledged her stiffly, and Julia went a violent, guilty red and could have died of mortification.

Andrew watched Richard disappear through the automatic doors. 'The great man himself, eh?' he laughed, an edge in the laugh and the comment. 'Well, I must dash, be in touch very soon,' he tossed over his shoulder as he set off at a sprint towards his car.

Brushing rain off the plain beige raincoat, Julia went inside, groaning inwardly at the awful quirk of timing which had brought Richard to the scene to spring her in that innocent embrace—and for good measure catch her out in her silly fib about her lunch partner. How on earth could she approach him about his plans for Dawlish after that?

The answer was, she simply couldn't, she told herself glumly as she headed to the cloakroom to hang up her coat and run a comb through her dampish hair. What *did* the fates have against her these days? she wondered pettishly, glaring at herself in the mirror while she jabbed on lipstick with an angry hand and then had to wipe it off where she had gone over the lip-line—and wipe the glare off her face as Eleanor came in, handbag over her shoulder, briefcase in hand and obviously about to leave for the afternoon.

'Oh, there you are, Julia,' she said in the tone of voice which implied she had been searching for Julia for hours. 'Richard's been asking to see you up in his office.'

'He can't have been asking for long since he's just come in himself,' Julia pointed out waspishly, annoyed at the tone of Eleanor's voice and at the not-very-subtle glance at the watch. Annoyed with the world at large and everybody in it, Richard Weldon most of all.

'Yes, well, do go up,' Eleanor said distractedly, while she burrowed in her handbag for something. 'Oh, and Julia,' she called to Julia at the door, 'I shan't be back this afternoon, so see Cliff if you have any problems.'

'Yes, all right,' muttered Julia, momentary pique quelling the nervousness at being summoned to Richard's office, something that had only happened once before—and then so he could take a bite out of her. He had no reason now to carpet her—not unless you counted her fib, and that would have been absurd. Yet why would he want to see her in his office when he had Cliff and Eleanor to provide the established line of management from the office floor to executive suite?

The answer to that came to her in the lift. . .a tentative trickle of an idea at first, but one which gathered momentum with every floor closer to the executive suite, so that by the end of the short trip to the fifth floor Julia was absolutely convinced Richard wanted to discuss the Dawlish managership with her. It must have been why he had invited her to lunch; it had been that sort of invitation, Julia decided in retrospect—definitely non-personal. Business. Of course, it had to be Dawlish. Julia could hardly suppress her excitement or her smile as she presented herself to his secretary—another middle-aged woman. Did Richard have something against young secretaries, or didn't he trust himself with them? In her giddy new mood, she nearly giggled at the notion.

He was on the telephone when the secretary showed her in. Her fib, and the kiss he had embarrasingly witnessed, completely out of her mind, Julia flashed him a brilliant smile as Richard motioned her to the chair in front of his desk. She sat down, and watched his scowl darken as he listened to whatever was being said on the other end of the line.

'Then see to it. I want an answer by the end of the day,' he snapped, and made her quite glad she was not at the receiving end of the intimidating bark.

He looked intimidating too, and off-puttingly remote behind the expanse of lovely pale wood set at an angle to one corner of the enormous uncluttered office, which could have accommodated half of Dawlish's little 'boxes' and still had room to spare.

'Five o'clock, no later,' Richard said curtly—a goodbye, as it turned out, since he simply ended the conversation by putting the telephone down. Julia felt the first stirrings of apprehension as she studied him carrying on as if she weren't in the room, jotting figures on to a pad in front of him for what seemed an age.

His jottings finally completed, and her apprehension well and truly entrenched, Richard looked up at her, and the last of Julia's delicious fantasy that this interview was going to be to her advantage vanished with that look—would have vanished with the cold, impersonal stare he had given her when she walked in, if only she had read it without her head in the clouds.

'That was Andrew Reith you were embracing on my doorstep, wasn't it?' he queried icily.

Granted, her expectations of an offer of branch managership had dissolved in the last thirty seconds, but Julia was not expecting anything like this. She stared blankly, and then, only because she was so surprised, she nodded. 'How did you know it was Andrew?' And could she have asked anything more irrelevant or stupid? she thought when she realised what she had said.

Richard considered her and the question without replying immediately, then he shrugged as if it was no great deal to satisfy her curiosity. 'He applied to Weldons for a job some time ago—when he was leaving Dawlish, I believe. I didn't take him on,' he informed her carelessly, unintentionally explaining Andrew's comment about second interviews, and his slightly odd attitude when he had learnt that Julia was at Weldons. Envy. . .?

'Types like that burn themselves out too quickly.' Richard was putting into words the feeling Julia herself had sometimes had about Andrew's very frenetic energy. 'I don't like it,' he said coldly, and for an instant she thought he meant Andrew's nerviness, which of course he didn't. 'And I won't have my staff fraternising with the opposition—if "fraternising" is the word for your passionate embrace,' he qualified with an icy sneer.

CHAPTER FIVE

'IT WAS not passionate!' Julia flung back hotly, inanely latching on to that before anything else.

A black eyebrow arched into a sneer. 'No. . .? How very disappointing for you! However——'

'However,' Julia snatched the word from him, 'it is none of your damned business. And as for "fraternising——"'

'Very much my business,' Richard finished for her with a bark. 'And no wonder you had to lie about who you were lunching with.' He watched the colour rush into her face and seemed to enjoy it. 'Andrew Reith was taken on by Fenwick and Jeffcott, who at this moment happen to be tendering for the same warehouse conversion that this company has already tendered for. *That* puts your relationship with Mr Reith into the category of a conflict of interest, and, since *my* interests are affected, I strongly suggest you review that relationship. Put bluntly, Miss Radcliffe, I won't stand for it.'

Julia found it difficult to believe her ears. Could this hard-headed, successful businessman—intelligent man, she had always assumed—possibly be serious? She had never heard such arrant nonsense in her life. Yes, she had told the silly white lie for reasons so irrational they couldn't hold up to scrutiny, but not out of subterfuge as Richard was implying. Two insignificant negotiators who wouldn't have the remotest clue what their principals were planning to tender for, constitute a case of conflict of interest by meeting for a pub lunch. . .? Of fraternisation by dint of exchanging a quick, friendly kiss. . .? Julia wanted to laugh, and did give an involuntary little cackle, then, amazed to realise she was still sitting there—meekly, Richard no doubt thought—she stood up, glaring contempt as his eyes dropped on cue to follow her hand as it smoothed the skirt over her slim hips.

The dark eyes swept back up, male eyes. . . hostile, yes, but the glitter in their angry depths had nothing to do with business. Julia felt a shock of recognition as new heat flooded into her cheeks. Small wonder she hadn't been able to make sense of this interview—supposedly about business ethics, when all along it had been a simple, very basic male-female confrontation. Male ego had been pricked; she had preferred lunch with insignificant Andrew Reith to big-time Richard Weldon. It would have been amusing and a wonderful boost to her own ego, if not so infuriating. Fraternisation, my eye! Richard would never have dared carpet a male negotiator he happened to see with 'the opposition'—unless in the unlikely event that the two men had been embracing on his doorstep.

Tempted for a moment to point out that little bit of sexual discrimination to him, Julia changed her mind. 'Your charge is absurd, Mr Weldon, and your subsequent "suggestion" even more so. I reject them both,' she told him, not with the fury raging inside her, but with a frigid disdain, and had the satisfaction of noting the swift surge of dark colour up the column of Richard's throat which gave the impression that his lovely maroon silk tie had all at once become too tight.

Then she walked out on him—not stormed out, walked out, coolly and calmly, and with wonderful dignity considering she was so furious with him she could barely see straight, and literally walked into Mike Tremayne's arms just inside the door of the branch when she got downstairs.

'Julia! Just the person I wanted to see,' he laughed when she had extricated herself out of his arms. 'Have you got anything booked for four-thirty?' he asked, and in her high-voltage mood Julia actually thought he was about to line her up for a date. 'I need a favour,' Mike went on, frowning a little at the glare she was presenting him. 'I need someone to go and meet a client at the Tower Views complex—apartment eight. You showed it to someone the other day, didn't you?'

Julia nodded, hurriedly replacing the glare with a look of interest once she realised Mike meant business. He was Eleanor's counterpart, a senior negotiator in charge of another group, and, while he had always been friendly towards her, they had never really had anything much to do with each other.

'I'd lined up Tom, but now it turns out he won't be back in time and the others are all booked up too, so I thought. . . I know Eleanor isn't in, but I'm sure she wouldn't mind you going for me.'

'Who is it? Can I have a look at the file?' Julia requested briskly.

'Er. . .there isn't one, actually. He hasn't been in here yet.' Mike gave an abrupt, defensive laugh.

'Look, I know this is a bit irregular, but I took the call myself and the chap sounded on the level. Paul Clarke—with an "e",' he added as if that 'e' settled the matter of Mr Clarke's bona fides. 'However, if you feel nervous about going off to meet him. . .' He trailed off with a cunning wave of the sexist flag, and got the knee-jerk response he was after.

'Don't be ridiculous—of course I'll go,' Julia snapped on cue. Meeting unknown clients off the premises was not all that irregular around Weldons; she knew most of the chaps were prepared to meet anyone anywhere if they sensed a sale, and for all she knew the same could have applied to Eleanor and the other two female negotiators.

Sneaky point won and goal achieved, Mike grinned. 'Great. Thanks. I told him four forty-five. He'll be waiting under the awning to the entrance of Building Three.'

Only Mr Paul Clarke—with an 'e'—wasn't waiting, nor was he anywhere in sight twenty minutes after the appointed time. Julia sat in her car in the small visitors' parking bay at one end of the paved courtyard. She could see anyone driving in through the gates and had a full view of the three buildings that made up this particular complex. They were all newly built, as opposed to being converted warehouses, but in keeping with the general style of the genuine articles—big and grim as far as Julia was concerned, and the longer she studied them the more she disliked them.

At ten past five she got out of the car, intending to check inside the building just in case Paul Clarke had mysteriously let himself in, and then realised his car would have been in the car park, which it wasn't. In fact, other than her own, there wasn't a car anywhere, and no people either. The courtyard was deserted and only the foyers and staircases of the buildings showed lights, not surprisingly, since the people who lived here worked—and long hours, by the look of it, to be able to afford these pricey pieces of trendy property. Young. . .career-orientated. Like herself. Were they. . .? Julia thought of her own mews house and the friendliness of the neighbourhood—a community in itself and utterly unlike this vase anonymous complex and the complex alongside—and alongside that, *ad infinitum*, it seemed.

The place was starting to give her the creeps. She wished someone would turn up—anyone, to allay the fanciful feeling that she was the only soul around for miles. She was cold too, loitering beside the car. It wasn't raining at the moment, but the skies were dark and scowling with the threat of a downpour and making it appear much later than it actually was. Julia peered at her watch again. Five more minutes and she would leave; half an hour was long enough to wait for anyone.

To give herself something to do, she walked down the paved pathway between two of the buildings, and was almost at the end of it when she thought she heard a car door slam in the parking bay she had just left. About to hurry back, she hesitated. Don't be stupid, she told herself as the shiver of alarm shot through her.

'Julia! Julia, where are you?'

It was not Paul Clarke, because, aside from the fact that he would not have known he was supposed to be meeting Julia Radcliffe, the urgent voice was unmistakable, although what its owner was doing here was beyond her. Julia took her time going back up the path, reaching the front of the buildings as Richard came at a run around the corner of one of them—after a frantic tear around the entrance of it, by the sound of the footsteps that had clattered echoingly all over the place. They collided, and he grabbed her arm to steady her after having half knocked her off her feet.

'Come to check that I'm not having a secret assignation with the opposition, I presume?' Julia taunted, shaken by the collision and the relief she felt that another human being had finally materialised, but not so shaken she didn't remember she was furious with him.

Richard gave an exasperated hiss through his teeth. 'What the hell are you doing here?' he demanded, shaking her in the violent grip.

'What are you? And let go of me, damn it, you're hurting me!' Julia ended in a yelp.

'Sorry,' Richard muttered, letting go of her arm, and then bellowed in the next breath, 'What in blazes do you mean, coming here alone at this time of evening to meet a man you don't know from a bar of soap?'

'How do you know I haven't met Paul Clarke?' Julia countered peevishly, giving her arm a rub where his fingers had dug in through her raincoat.

'I know because Mike Tremayne told me,' he told her angrily. 'And I told Mike Tremayne a few things in return,' he added savagely, and made Julia feel sorry for poor Mike and angrier still with Richard for making an issue out of something some of his staff probably did every day of the week.

'So you know what I'm doing here. What are you? Assuming you're not tailing me in the hope of catching me "fraternising" again,' Julia jeered, and didn't catch the return mutter in full, but the part she did catch sounded like 'looking out for idiotic females'.

'What! Are you telling me you've come here especially to ensure that no one abducts me?' Her voice rose dangerously in shrill, disbelieving anger.

'Frankly, it'd be a relief if someone did,' Richard growled, not denying her accusation, Julia noted, and she needed a moment to take it in—that he had come rushing over to play 'minder'. And then she didn't like it, not one bit. The gratuitous chivalry—whatever—was an insult to her professionalism, not to mention would make her a laughing stock among her colleagues if they ever found out about it.

'How dare you. . .? How dare you show me up like this?' Julia could have wept with rage.

Richard's face glowered angry surprise at her, and that made her want to hit him out of sheer frustration at his obtuseness. 'How do you think this is going to make me look back at the office? A silly little twit of a female, too incompetent to be let out alone, that's how!' she flung at him in a wail.

'Oh, for heaven's sake!' Richard ground out in exasperation. 'Must you over-react to everything? There happens to be a rule in my organisation that applies to female negotiators—and I don't care if it's sexist, so don't bother drawing it to my attention,' he pre-empted her retort testily. 'That rule is: they don't go out to meet clients unknown—not morning, noon or night. It's obviously being flouted behind my back, but I'll soon see to that,' Richard threatened ominously. 'You know perfectly well that every responsible agency has the policy now, you dug your heels in about it at Dawlish yourself—enjoyed doing it too,' he threw in with snide accuracy. 'And if you weren't scared stiff hanging around this spooky place, then you damned well should have been. Any sensible person would have been—yes, me too,' he admitted in a snarl before she had a chance to toss in a jeer, although actually Julia was too taken aback by his vehemence to have come up with one. Richard took her arm again, not quite in the same punishing grip, but almost. 'Come on, you're not waiting around here a moment longer.' He started marching her across the courtyard to their cars. All the automatically set lamps had switched themselves on, but there was still an eeriness about the place that came from its echoing emptiness. 'And if you ever try to——' Richard broke off his growl as a late-model BMW came screeching in through the gateway, slowed, then cruised into the parking bay as they reached it.

'Mr Clarke with an "e",' muttered Julia, freeing her arm of Richard's hold to take a look at her watch. 'And only forty minutes late.'

The driver got out, a tall, slim man; late twenties and expensively dressed in an ultra-conservative way that was possibly the height of fashion among his set.

Richard looked as if he was ready to tell Paul Clarke to go to hell, but then the passenger-side door opened and a woman got out. 'Damn,' he muttered under his breath.

The young man hurried around the car to them. 'I say, sorry if we're a little late. We got held up. You *are* the Weldons people, aren't you? Paul Clarke.' He shot a hand out to Richard, who had no choice but to take it.

'Weldon,' he returned coldly. 'And this is Miss Radcliffe, who's been waiting for you.'

'Oh, quite.' Paul Clarke jerked a mechanical smile at her but didn't offer his hand, and Julia didn't offer hers. 'My wife, Liz,' he nodded offhandedly at the plump young woman standing nervously beside the car, and only then did the charmless Mr Clarke seem to realise that 'the Weldons people' were not exactly bubbling over with joy at his arrival. 'I say, we can still look the place over, can't we? You weren't about to leave, were you?'

'No, of course not,' Julia assured him hurriedly before Richard could answer. 'If you'll come this way,' she invited brusquely, and started to walk towards Building Three. In a moment, Mrs Clarke had caught up with her. Julia didn't look around to see if Paul Clarke was following.

'It was awfully good of you to wait,' Liz Clarke said apologetically in a soft, little-girl voice. 'Paul was running late in picking me up and I honestly didn't think you'd still be here, but he said. . . Anyway, I'm sorry,' she mumbled, not finishing what Paul had said. Julia could guess: something like 'of course they'll wait, that's what they're paid for.'

'That's all right,' she said, not unkindly, since it was clear who called the shots in this duo and she felt sorry for any woman unlucky enough to be Paul Clarke's wife.

She had thought Liz Clarke merely plump, but in the brighter light of the foyer Julia saw it wasn't plumpness under the camel-hair coat, but obvious pregnancy. She swung her eyes away, aware that she must have stared at the poor woman in horror. What on earth was she doing inspecting a Docklands apartment where babies had been the very last thing in the developer's mind? Not even the very last— simply non-existent.

The apartment was on the second floor, and as they walked up the showy, classy curve of stairway, carpeted in ice-pale grey, Julia went through the motions of pointing out the various features, mentioning the swimming-pool and sauna housed in the next building but available to all the residents of the complex. 'I'm afraid there isn't any room for a push-chair in here. These apartments were not really designed for young familes,' she pointed out the obvious with a rueful smile as they entered the sleekly stark apartment.

'I know.' Liz's big brown eyes looked teary. 'I've told Paul that I'll hate it here, but he said I could stand it for a year or two and then he can sell up and make an enormous profit.'

The last bit was true, but at what price? His wife and baby isolated. . .neighbours out at work; no kindly, middle-aged busybodies popping in to see how a new mother was coping and doing the odd bit of shopping for her; a husband who probably didn't come home till all hours like the rest of the dwellers in these apartments. It made Julia shudder to think what a miserable time Liz Clarke would have of it. It apparently made Liz Clarke shudder too.

'I'll hate it, I know I will!' she wailed piteously in that small-girl voice. 'It's wrong for us. You think that too, don't you, Miss Radcliffe?'

'I. . .well, yes, I suppose I do,' Julia admitted reluctantly, forced into the truth by the appeal in the tearful brown eyes.

'Then please tell him,' Liz begged like a child; she looked not much past childhood. . .eighteen, nineteen at the most, Julia would have guessed. 'Paul won't listen to me, he might to you.'

'Mrs Clarke, you know I can't do that. You'll have to work it out between you,' Julia said firmly.

They both turned towards the door as Paul Clarke's voice rang out in the hall. . .rang out everywhere in a high-pitched enthusiasm. It was 'super layout, super décor, super fittings.' Anyone would have taken him for an over-the-top salesman. Julia couldn't hear Richard at all. The two men eventually appeared in the doorway of the small room—the second bedroom, where she and Liz were talking.

'Perhaps you and your wife would like to look around together,' Richard suggested with frosty politeness. 'Miss Radcliffe and I can——' He was cut off by Liz Clarke's lunge towards her husband.

'Miss Radcliffe doesn't think this is suitable for us either, Paul,' she burst out, startling her husband, and Julia even more. 'Do you, Miss Radcliffe?' She swung to Julia for support.

Julia kept her gaze on the couple, not daring to meet Richard's eye. 'I think perhaps you may not have fully considered all the implications of living in this particular location,' she said tightly, looking Paul Clarke steadily in the eye.

He took a moment to react, then the lip went up in a sneer. 'Do you now, Miss Radcliffe? And who asked you to butt in?' He threw a flushed glare at Richard, who was silently propping up the doorway and looking too bored for words. 'I thought your sales staff are supposed to sell.'

'Oh, they are, and believe me they do,' Richard drawled, ice under the surface of the words. 'I only employ the best, so you might do well to consider Miss Radcliffe's expert judgement.'

Julia was not sure she heard right, and neither was Paul Clarke. They both stared at Richard blankly.

'I know that our other branches can offer you more suitable properties which are just as appealing. . .' Julia recovered herself to attempt a rescue of the situation, but was too late.

'Come on, Liz,' Paul Clarke was snarling at his poor wife. 'We're getting out of here. I'm not going to be told what I should be buying by this lot!'

Richard politely stood aside from the doorway so they could charge out, and after a few moments the Clarkes' hurrying footsteps could be heard echoing loudly across the courtyard. Two doors slammed; the BMW roared into life and roared out of the courtyard. After that it was very quiet again.

Chin up defiantly, Julia turned from gazing absently out of the window and met Richard's eyes. Now for it; the show of loyalty was over—had to be, because, while she had appreciated his unexpected support in front of the client, she wasn't so naïve as to think she was going to escape the deferred tongue-lashing now the Clarkes were off the premises.

'She was pregnant,' she got in first, defensively, and was not prepared for the small, wry smile.

'Actually, I had managed to work that out for myself,' Richard returned drily.

'Then you should also have managed to work out that this——' Julia flapped an angry hand at the room '—is no place for a baby or a new mother.'

'And that matters to you?' Richard's voice was curiously soft.

Of course it matters, Julia didn't bother saying, because he would not have understood. She gave an abrupt shrug and turned her back on him to stare out of the window again at the bleak, windswept courtyard.

'You don't like them at all, do you?' Richard had come up beside her.

She half turned to him. 'The Clarkes? He was a——'

'He was a bully, and one would be hard-pressed to want to sell him a tent if his house burnt down, we can agree on that,' Richard interposed his contemptuous opinion of their erstwhile client before she got hers out. 'But I'm not talking about the Clarkes, I'm talking about these Dockland estates. They're not your scene at all, are they?'

Strange, how everybody seemed to arrive at that conclusion: Moira. . . Andrew, now Richard—Cliff would sooner or later too, thought Julia, a little taken aback, and, while her first instinct was to try and bluff her way out, lie through her teeth, she ended up giving another shrug and a flat, unelaborated 'No.'

What was the point of lying? Richard couldn't sack her just because she didn't like what she was selling—not unless her feelings interfered with the selling, and after this evening's fiasco they would never do that again. Investments, not homes, was to be the name of the game from now on, and who was she to cast aspersions on the likes of Paul Clarke when she was in her third house in six years? Even speculators had their reasons.

'Well, that's being honest.'

Richard didn't add 'for once', but it was left hanging off the end of the sentence, and not without reason, Julia had to admit, since it seemed she was forever fibbing to him about one thing or another: Andrew today, Dawlish the previous time. Dawlish—Richard's new branch. Could she ask him about it now? Julia hesitated and missed her chance.

'Come on, we're getting out of here,' Richard repeated Paul Clarke's exit line, and, having anticipated probing about her dislike of the Docklands and/or a tart reminder that she was not employed as a social worker, Julia was relieved, but too distracted to wonder why Richard was letting the matter drop, or why he didn't say anything more as they locked up and started down the stairs.

'You've bought Dawlish, haven't you?' She came out with the question when they were crossing the spacious foyer downstairs, not really asking, but accusing—and very belligerently in her nervousness.

'Where did you hear that?' Richard returned casually, giving her a quick glance but without any surprise in it.

'Around,' Julia equivocated. 'What does it matter where I heard it? Is it true?'

'Yes, it's true.' Richard held the front door open for her and she gave a shiver as they emerged into the freezing courtyard after the warmth of the centrally-heated building. Richard lifted an arm as if to put it around her shoulder, then seemed to think better of it and dropped it to his side.

'You might have told me,' Julia muttered. 'You must have known how interested I'd be.'

'Really?' he countered. 'Then you must have revised your thoughts about Dawlish very recently, since I seem to remember you going to great lengths to convince me that you'd outgrown it. . .become what was it? Stale. . .jaded? I can't recall the exact words.'

He could recall them all right. 'I lied and you know it,' Julia confessed through her teeth, and was chagrined by the soft, smug chuckle.

'Do I? Anyway, I'm glad you've brought up the subject, because I've been meaning to sound you out about various aspects of my plans for Dawlish—like the managership, for instance,' Richard threw in chattily, and was ready with the faint quizzical smile when she swung her eyes to him in wild disbelief. 'Interested, Julia?' It sounded suspiciously like a taunt.

Julia nodded, slowly, distrustfully, yet in spite of herself a hundred little flares of hope leapt inside her willy-nilly. Was it just possible he was serious. . .that she really had a chance of being offered the managership? 'Yes, I'm interested,' she said warily, translating the nodding into speech.

'I thought you might be. In fact,' Richard continued when they reached their cars, 'that's what I wanted to talk to you about over lunch today, only, of course, because of your prior engagement, I didn't get the chance. So what I suggest we do now is get out of this perishing cold and go and talk about it over an early dinner.' There was nothing at all suspicous about that; a reasonable suggestion, it seemed to Julia, until he added, 'And I'm sure you'll find "fraternising" with me much more enjoyable than with Andrew Reith,' and then the suggestion took on a whole new, nasty meaning, and Julia suddenly saw the light—or rather the cheese in the mousetrap. The hundred little flares of silly hope died an instantaneous death in the freeze that came over her.

'Don't you mean much more *rewarding*—to my career?' Her voice was brittle with icy contempt, her face a cold, tight mask as she watched a rapid succession of expressions fly across Richard's face. . .surprise and puzzlement, and finally a comprehension that held something unpleasant in it.

'Oh, that too, but only if you prove worth it, Julia,' he murmured with a soft, blatant suggestiveness that quite took her breath away and left her staring, half mesmerised as he put his forefinger to her lips and traced their outline lightly while looking at her through his lashes in a way that was positively lewd.

It was probably that awful look that finally brought a reaction from her; Julia slapped him unthinkingly, and so hard her palm stung from the contact with his cheek, and then, from the look on his face and the raised hands, she thought he was going to slap her right back and tried to step out of range, only she didn't make it. The hands clapped over her ears, pulling her face forward, and head almost off her neck, and Richard kissed her instead, if that was the word for the enraged ramming of mouth against mouth—physical assault by any other name, and so painful that after the first shocked second Julia's lips went numb and her mind into a freeze.

Seconds—or was it minutes?—later, Richard released her with a suddenness that almost threw her off balance, swung around to his Rover, slammed himself into it, then wrenched the engine on and took off out of the courtyard in a roaring exit Paul Clarke would have envied.

Julia was shaking so much she had to lean against her car, while in blurred rage she rummaged frenziedly in her bag for the car key, the only wild thought in her mind to chase Richard through the Docklands, ram him to a stop and scream at him— more than scream; a flurry of homicidal fantasies had him lying dead at her feet, and even that was not nearly satisfying enough, although by the time she'd found her keys, dropped them twice, and finally got herself into the car, the idea had lost its momentum. Not so her fury.

Who did he think he was to behave like that? Who did he think she was to be treated like that prop ositioned, all but assaulted, then flung off as if she was beneath contempt—as if *she* had insulted *him*, when he should have been grovelling apologies for daring to imply she would stoop so low as to trade favours for the Dawlish managership. That was what he had meant, wasn't it? Of course it was; if there had been a skerrick of doubt, his last taunt had dispensed with it. If she was worth it. What else could it mean? Was that how people—women—got managerships in his organisation? Julia could hardly believe it of him—that Richard would resort to such low-down tactics when he could have probably had any woman he wanted for the asking or charming, anyway. Except Julia Radcliffe.

Was that what it was all about? Her initial responsiveness towards him notwithstanding, she had not turned out to be the push-over Richard had anticipated, and it must have rankled more than she imagined. Look at the way he had reacted over Andrew—with pure, unadulterated macho jealousy, the irony being that she would sooner have gone to lunch with Richard than Andrew, and, more ironic still, would have accepted the dinner invitation tonight—or any night, if he hadn't dangled the managership as implied bait. Why? Because over the last three and a half weeks, she had reached the stage of liking him. . .enjoying his company without feeling threatened by him. In other words, fallen for his ploy to lull her into a false sense of security, more fool her.

Well, he would never get the chance to take her for that again, Julia vowed, feeling something harden inside her, and for a moment she thought of her mother almost with understanding.

CHAPTER SIX

THREE viewings—one of which had ended in an offer, and, surprisingly, all three a breeze. Or perhaps not so surprisingly. Julia was conscious of a surge of confidence and a new, hard edge about herself the next day, as if the unpleasantness of the previous evening had snapped her back into the cool, determined detachment with which she had arrived at Weldons and the Docklands, and which had somehow become lost in a mish-mash of personal feelings about herself, Richard, clients, the job—everything, it seemed.

No more. All personal feelings were going to stay in suspended animation for the next two years; the clients at arm's length, and the job nothing more than the means to an end. Pile up the commissions and get the hell out of the place, and not even the prospect of coming face to face with Richard sooner or later could put a dint in her new, above-it-all attitude. Just to be on the safe side, though, Julia was very careful not to arrive at the car park anywhere near the time Richard usually did, and, whether by good luck or good management, there had not been an encounter for nearly two days.

Feeling pretty pleased with herself, she was returning from her last appointment about three-thirty on Friday afternoon, when the tall dark woman—'the

woman from Personnel', Julia had dubbed her—
called to her from one of the armchairs in the foyer.

'Julia, hello.'

Julia went over to her. They had seen each other
two or three times now in passing, but this time the
woman was obviously expecting Julia to stop and
talk.

'How are you these days?' The very attractive face,
mid-thirties at close range, radiated a lovely warm
smile, and to her embarrassment, Julia still couldn't
put a name to it.

'Fine. Great. Awfully busy. How are you?' Julia
laughed, exuding the extra-bright enthusiasm people
do when they're trying to cover up their awkward-
ness that they don't really know who they're talking
to.

'Oh, I'm probably as busy as you are,' the woman
laughed back. 'What with one thing and another—
you know how it is. I'm just waiting for Richard now
to come and see to some things for me,' she volunteered—as if it was of interest to Julia, the only
interest being, as far as Julia was concerned, to make
an exit before Richard actually materialised.

'That's great,' she enthused inanely, and started to
edge away, trying not to look too rude about it. 'If
you'll excuse me now, I——'

'What about getting together for lunch one day, to
catch up on things?'

What things? 'That would be lovely,' Julia murmured, determined to ask someone who this extra-
ordinarily friendly person was so she wouldn't feel
such an idiot the next time they came across each
other. 'I really must go,' she said hastily as she saw

Richard emerge from the Docklands branch and come towards them.

'Here's Richard!' the older woman exclaimed—as if Julia had missed seeing him.

'Yes,' Julia muttered, then looked right through him without a blink and with no acknowledgement of his surly nod as she walked past him and went into the branch.

Well, she had managed that quite commendably, she congratulated herself smugly at her desk. A few more passing-by encounters, and even having to talk to him wouldn't be too much of a strain—if she had to, and that wouldn't be often if she could help it.

She got out a folio of plans for a warehouse conversion that was in the pipeline; there were a few details she wanted to check with Eleanor before taking the folio home for the weekend to study the plans at her leisure. She unrolled the sheets and started flipping through them for the one she wanted, then stopped and glanced up as someone came around the screen.

'Eleanor, you've saved me a walk,' Julia greeted her supervisor cheerfully. 'I was going to come to talk to you about that last appointment, but I was just fishing out these plans first because I wanted to ask you about something I'm not clear about. . .' She recommenced the flipping.

'Don't bother hunting it up,' Eleanor forestalled her, an odd note in her voice, and when Julia looked up she found a matching odd expression on Eleanor's face, although what either signified she couldn't guess.

'And I shouldn't bother spending any more time on those plans at all.'

Puzzled, her hand stilled on the sheets, Julia watched Eleanor settle into the chair in front of the desk.

'You're being transferred out of the branch,' Eleanor informed her matter-of-factly, as if she was telling Julia the time of day. 'Cliff told me this afternoon. He'll want to see you later—to tell you himself, I expect,' she explained, the sharpness in her eyes giving away that she was not nearly so matter-of-fact about what she was saying as she was trying to make out. 'Oh, for heaven's sake, don't go all hysterical about it,' she reverted to her natural snappish self as Julia came out of the brief shock with a long peal of laughter.

It wasn't hysteria; she really did find it funny that Richard had scored his point so neatly—and had not wasted a moment about it either. . .paying her back for turning down his offer of the Dawlish manager-ship, long strings dangling. Even having witnessed her abysmal performance with the Clarkes, he couldn't risk pushing her out of the door in case she created a stink, but yes, he could push her out of the branch—into some deadwater pond of a branch where she would not last a month for boredom and lack of commissions. Her resignation guaranteed. Neat. Clever. She had to hand it to him.

'Did you ever want to be a branch manager, Eleanor?' she put to her supervisor, apropos of nothing, it must have seemed to Eleanor, whose face showed that she thought Julia was reacting more than just a little strangely to the news.

Eleanor gave a quick, almost spiteful smile. 'Is that where you thought you were heading?' she asked, spite threading the words. 'Well then, Miss Radcliffe, it looks as if you overestimated your own attractiveness, doesn't it? *I've* got the managership, if you really want to know.' She couldn't hold back the triumph from her voice. 'Yes, I thought that might surprise you,' she laughed as Julia's mouth fell open, 'but it seems that, when it comes to the crunch, Richard is not about to let his interest in a pretty face get in the way of sound business practice. I may not have your looks—and whatever other assets that don't get listed on CVs,' she tossed in nastily, 'but I've worked damned hard in this branch for three years, and *I* deserve the managership, not *you*. It was understood ages ago that I would be the one taking over from Cliff when he was moved on—to head the new Scottish division, as it happens, and—oh lord, what's the matter with you now?'

Julia was making funny little gurgling noises in her throat and shaking her head, but not managing to get out a word. Mild hysteria this time, maybe, as the penny finally dropped what Eleanor was talking about. And about a whole lot of other things that had puzzled her about her supervisor. . .the veiled hostility, the undercurrent of resentment. Poor Eleanor had been afraid she was about to have her prized job snatched from under her nose and a rank outsider handed the branch managership, just because Richard found her attractive! Ironically, Eleanor was not very far off the mark—if you disregarded the mix-up about branches.

Julia pulled herself together with an effort. 'Sorry,'

she mumbled, embarrassed by her own silly reaction. 'And congratulations. I'm sure you'll do a great job,' she added, and really meant it.

Nonplussed by the compliment, Eleanor flushed, looked suspicious for a moment, and then apparently decided to accept it—not quite gracefully. 'Yes. . .well, thanks,' she muttered, and gave a puzzled shake of the head. 'I can't make you out, Julia, you——' She cut herself off abruptly with a shrug and rose to her feet. 'You've been doing a really good job yourself lately,' she said grudgingly, and it must have cost her a lot. 'And I want you to know that I. . .well, that I didn't have anything to do with your transfer out of the branch.'

'Oh, I know that, Eleanor—believe me, I know,' Julia assured her with a sudden harsh bitterness.

Eleanor frowned, seemed about to ask something, then changed her mind. 'Anyway, Cliff will talk to you about it later.'

'Monday,' Julia said airily, taking her hand off the sheets of plans and letting them spring back into a roll. 'I feel like going home now, and yes, you can tell Cliff it's another headache, if you like,' she suggested with a grating giggle. 'And I'm not rostered on tomorrow,' she chatted on as she shoved papers into drawers and cleared the desk under Eleanor's startled gaze. 'So, you see, it'll have to be Monday.' She stood up, picked up her handbag from the floor and swung it over her shoulder. 'If I decide to come in at all, that is, and I'll be doing a lot of thinking about that!'

* * *

The front door buzzer started buzzing and stayed buzzing with someone's finger determined not to budge until she had come down and opened the door. The sound was unbearable after the first few seconds. Just out of the shower, Julia threw on her robe and came tearing out of the bathroom, almost tripping over the overnight bag she'd left on the landing on her return from her cousin's in Kent about half an hour earlier. It was after ten o'clock, she was dog-tired and not about to be at home to anybody.

She flung the door open with a bad-tempered flourish and the assault on her ears ceased as Richard removed his persistent finger from the buzzer.

'You should always ask who it is before you open the door to anyone at this hour of night,' he admonished in a mutter by way of greeting.

One hand on the doorknob, the other shooting to the top of her towelling robe and holding the fronts tightly together, Julia glared at him. 'Rest assured, Mr Weldon, I'd never have opened it to you at any hour, night or day.' She made to slam the door in his face, only Richard had obviously anticipated the move and the one foot already planted inside was deftly followed up with the other; a seasoned door-to-door salesman could not have made a better job of gaining entry where he wasn't wanted.

'If you've come to apologise. . .' Julia began belligerently, taking a hasty step back because the tiny entrance hall was not big enough for the two of them without their brushing against each other.

'Apologise? Didn't cross my mind. And I don't suppose it crossed yours that *you* might owe *me* an apology? Obviously not,' Richard muttered as Julia snorted in derision. 'Shall we go up? I want to talk to you and I'd rather not stand about down here. Besides, you'll catch cold with nothing on under that thing.' He let his eyes drift down to her hand at the lapels and gave a soft, malicious laugh as, on cue, Julia spun on her heel and started angrily up the stairs.

Had she really thought she could come face to face with him without turning a hair? That she had even calmed down about her 'transfer' during the two days she had spent with Derek and his family while coming to a decision to resign? Yes, she really had thought that. Now, one look at the man responsible for all the hassles in her life and it was back to square one; the fury that had made her want to kill him in the Tower View car park was back with a vengeance. And he wanted an apology from her? For what? Slapping his face?

'Been away for the weekend?'

Julia pushed the overnight bag into the bedroom and slammed the door on it without bothering to confirm his observation.

'I wondered where you'd got to,' Richard went on with spurious chattiness, following her across the landing. 'I've been in the area quite a bit this weekend and passed by several times. I just happened to be passing by again when I saw your lights on.'

The mews house he was buying was virtually around the corner; his girlfriend might have already moved in if completion had been effected as early as the owner had wanted. Why else would Richard be hanging around the area? Julia contemplated him coldly, not believing for a moment the 'just happened to be passing by', and not about to believe any explanation he might be about to trot out regarding her 'transfer', so-called.

They were in the living-room. . .small, like every room in the house, and pretty and chintzy. Richard looked completely out of place. Out of 'uniform' in casual navy pullover over dark trousers, he still looked somehow too formidable—too big and dark for her feminine environment. Too male, thought Julia, suddenly very anxious to get him out of it.

She didn't invite him to sit down to ensure that he left all the quicker, and it was Sunday anyway, and her own house, her own time; Richard was an intruder on all counts and employee-employer rules didn't apply, nor did normal civilities, after his behaviour in the Docklands car park on Wednesday night.

Uptight and angry, she watched him stroll about the room, glancing here and there—at the bookshelves, the records, then going over to the large window and giving the curtains a proprietorial tug together where they hadn't quite met in the centre. Very much at home—in her home; Julia couldn't stand it a moment more. 'Whatever it is you've barged into my house at midnight to tell me, I suggest you tell me, and get out.'

Richard tossed a glance at his watch as he turned to her. '"Midnight" and "barged", is exaggerating it, but then exaggeration is your forte, isn't it? And I had to come here because you weren't in the office yesterday and I——'

'I wasn't rostered on,' Julia broke in to defend

herself heatedly, momentarily forgetting she had resolved never to go back to Weldons again.

'No, you weren't, as I found out when I came looking for you yesterday morning.'

'Then you shouldn't have put yourself to the trouble, because Eleanor had already told me about my imminent "transfer". Julia dripped acid with the word.

'Yes, I gathered Ms Bradley let the cat out of the bag—or as little as she knew of it. A fine example of the sisterhood sticking together.'

'It needs to, with men like you around,' Julia hissed back scathingly, keeping Eleanor's less-than-altruistic motives to herself, then, trying to look casual about it, took herself rather quickly to the other side of the kitchen counter as Richard came across the room.

The counter a barrier between them, he stopped on his side of it and studied her in a mixture of amusement and irritation. 'You have the vilest temper to go with that beautiful red hair. Yes, it is beautiful.' He nodded as Julia's hand shot mechanically to her hair, pinned up haphazardly after the shower. She snatched her hand away at the gratuitous compliment, taking in a quick check of the fronts of her robe before dropping it to her side. 'Everything is quite concealed. Not a peep,' Richard reassured her sarcastically. 'Come to think of it, I believe I've mentioned your temper before, haven't I? But I don't think I fully realised the mind-boggling capacity for jumping to conclusions that goes with it—about me, for instance—and I don't like it.' Richard's voice hardened; the sarcastic banter went out it, and the amusement out of his face. 'I don't take kindly to anyone all but accusing me of selling managerships to my female employees for favours and——'

'If the cap fits!' Julia interjected with a spurt of venom.

'You'd better explain yourself, Julia.' Hands on the counter, Richard suddenly leaned threateningly over it, forcing her to take a couple of jerky steps back.

'You said——' she began, and stopped to adjust the robe slipping off her shoulder.

'Yes? What did I say?' Richard challenged, ignoring her agitated grab at the robe.

Distracted for a moment, Julia lost her venom. 'About fraternising. . .' she mumbled, trying to remember his exact words '. . .that I'd find it more enjoyable with you than with Andrew.'

'And so you would!' he barked, straightening up and glaring at her. 'But, lord help me, all I was doing was taking a dig at myself for being such an idiot over you and Reith. . .all that rubbish I talked about fraternisation. That's why I wanted to catch you that evening at the office—to apologise, only Tremayne told me he'd sent you to Tower Views, so I had to come over there. I didn't get a chance to explain or apologise because you instantly jumped to your nasty conclusions and made out that I was the last of the casting-couch directors, or whatever.'

Julia gave a snort of a laugh. 'Don't try back-pedalling to make it seem I misinterpreted you, because you practically spelt it out for me just to make sure I hadn't misinterpreted you.' She reminded him indignantly.

'All right,' Richard conceded with a glower and a dismissive shrug. 'I played along with your horrid little assumption—but only because I was so furious I could have strangled you, and if you ever slap me again. . .' He left the threat hanging in the air just long enough for Julia to feel the impact of that furious, punishing kiss. 'However, I didn't come to tell you I don't like being slapped,' he went on. 'I came to explain that you're being transferred out of the Dockland branch because I want you in the Dawlish branch—as manager, and I figured I'd better tell you that before you got it into that obstinate head never to set foot in Weldons again. And if you tell me that particular train of thought hadn't entered your melodramatic little mind, I wouldn't believe you. You've got storming out in a huff down to an art form.'

Julia ignored everything except the bit sandwiched in the middle—the Dawlish managership—and, in spite of herself, there they were again, those willy-nilly flares of hope. Staring back distrustfully, she waited for the punchline that would kill off those damned hopes once and for all.

'Well?'

'The managership on what conditions?' she asked point-blank, and almost winced as Richard slapped himself on the side of the head in frustration.

'Here we go again? Can't you ever take anything on face-value?' he growled. 'What conditions do you expect? That you jump into bed with me every afternoon at four o'clock?' he flung at her in angry sarcasm, and she flushed beetroot at the crudeness of the taunt. 'Honestly, Julia, you're so distrustful, it would be funny, if it weren't so damned insulting. I assure you that when I want a woman in my bed I don't need to resort to buying one.'

With that super ego and those looks, that had to be true. So, maybe no strings, but Julia was still a long way from clicking her heels in the air. 'Why me? For Dawlish?'

'Because that's what you were hired for,' Richard told her impatiently. 'To be transferred back to the Dawlish branch as soon as the deal was through.'

'I was?'

'You didn't think we snapped you up for the Docklands, did you?' Richard retorted with a laugh. 'Oh, I'm not saying you've not made a reasonable job of it—especially given your distaste for it. In fact, Eleanor thinks you've done quite well—Cliff too, but then they weren't around at the Clarkes' viewing, were they? No, I'm not sniping, I'm just telling you you're not quite the actress you thought you were, and the Docklands, as you admitted yourself, are not your scene, whereas mews and mansion flats are. So you're being sent back there, and I'd have thought you'd jump at the chance.'

Julia would have thought that too, if there hadn't been five weeks of Richard Weldon to confuse every thought in her head. 'Then why didn't you—Cliff, rather—tell me what the plans were right from the start, when he offered me the job after the second interview?'

'Because things weren't quite in place re the Dawlish deal and, since you'd already resigned from Dawlish at the end of your tether, our idea was to put you on ice at the Docklands, where you insisted you wanted to be, until the Dawlish business was finalised. If we hadn't taken you on when we did, then you'd have gone off somewhere else, wouldn't you?'

'I suppose so,' Julia had to agree reluctantly. A sudden thought struck her. 'Had you already started negotiations when you came to Dawlish to view Chiswell Mews?'

'I'd expressed interest—just,' Richard admitted grudgingly.

'Then why couldn't you have told me then?' she demanded angrily.

'Sounds of hollow laughter.' Richard matched the words with a hollow laugh. 'For heaven's sake, Julia, you'd have run a mile if you'd had the faintest inkling you'd end up working for me—at Dawlish, the Docklands or anywhere else. You resigned the instant you found out as it was, didn't you?'

'I. . .'

'And changed your mind, of course. Now, do you want the job or don't you?' he demanded testily. 'Surely, as far as your career plans go, managing a branch is going to suit you right down to the ground—a sort of dry run at my expense before you venture out on your own.'

'How do you know what my plans are?' Julia took him up on the sarcastic point in peevish surprise.

'Top secret, were they?' Richard grinned wolfishly. 'Some secret, when two minutes in your company and anybody with a glass eye and half an ounce of business acumen could see what you're all about, biting the bullet and counting the days—and the money—before you can go off to do your own thing.' Strangely, he didn't seem to resent what she was 'all about'. 'Come on, Julia, admit it; you'd give your eye-teeth to have a go at mangaging Dawlish the way you think it should be managed.'

'Just my teeth,' Julia said tightly through her teeth.

One of the dark expressive eyebrows rose mockingly while Richard seem to consider her answer before giving a light laugh. 'Whatever you say.' He allowed her the point carelessly. 'But since you mentioned them—conditions—I do actually have a set of them for you, and before you whizz to your conclusions about that,' he smiled tartly as her face went into a pinch, 'what I mean is that, since we're going to be coming across each other at the odd meetings and discussion session, I want courteous, friendly co-operation from you. I mean it, Julia. I won't stand for you jumping down my throat every time I open my mouth, or any temper tantrums, or storming out of——'

'I wouldn't be so damned unprofessional!' Julia burst out indignantly, highly insulted he was implying she might start a slanging match in the middle of a meeting. 'I would never allow personal feelings to intrude into business matters,' she declared with self-righteous pompousness as she emerged from behind the counter, then had the grace to blush under the frankly sceptical gaze. 'Anyway, I assure you you'll have all the courteous, friendly co-operation you require from me at all times,' she finished huffily, and realised she had just accepted the job.

'What a little stoic!' Richard exclaimed tartly. 'Prepared to lay down arms and be civil to me in the interests of furthering your career, are you?'

'Yes,' Julia retorted shortly.

'Is that career really so important to you?'

What was it in his voice. . .an edge of anger? Disapproval? Whatever it was, it hit a raw nerve. 'What if it is? she countered hotly, and was annoyed at the defensiveness in her own voice, and then infuriated at the way Richard was shaking his head in a 'more in sorrow than anger' act.

'There are other things in life than career and getting to the top of the professional tree, Julia.'

Not for her there wasn't—not for a long time. Career meant independence, and that was the most important thing in the world, but she owed Richard Weldon no explanation or justification of her single-mindedness. 'Spare me the homilies, I'm not interested. And anyway, you don't know what you're talking about,' she added in a mutter, wanting an end to the unwelcome turn the conversation had suddenly taken into the personal.

'Oh yes, I do!' Richard returned with a flash of unmistakable anger in his eyes. 'And you know I'm right, for all your expertise in self-deception, and your remarkable capacity for twisting things around when you're too scared to face them the way they really are. Take me, for example—careful, you'll go crosseyed with that glare,' he warned sarcastically. 'Face it, Julia, I've managed to get under your skin—broken through the six-foot barricade you've built around yourself to shut men out, to shut me out, and, my sweet, all that hostility towards me is only your defence mechanism working overtime. You're attracted to me and feel threatened, terrified, in fact, that, great career plans notwithstanding, you'll start responding like a woman to a man who finds you

very attractive, very desirable, and who wants you.'
He reached out and caught her by the arm as she
swung away on a wave of sheer fright. 'And whom
you've been encouraging in your own sweet, naïve
way,' he finished with the preposterous comment
that would have stopped her in her tracks even
without his grip on her arm.

'Encourage you? Me? Don't you ever get tired of
flattering yourself?' Squeaky with disbelief, her voice
was barely up to the taunt.

'And don't *you* ever get tired of lying to yourself?'
Richard mocked back. 'Who changed their routine to
turn up at the car park at ten past eight practically
every morning for over three weeks? Not me, Julia; I
didn't change my schedule from eight-thirty to ten
past, nor back again to eight-thirty at the end of the
last week. All coincidence, was it, and nothing to do
with you wanting to spend some time with me?' He
put a palm to her burning cheek. 'Now try to lie your
way out of that.'

Julia couldn't; yet couldn't believe she had been
arranging the 'coincidences', and even if she had, it
had been so subconsciously she hadn't been aware
of what she was doing—not until the last couple of
days perhaps, when she had deliberately gone out of
her way to avoid him. Mortified, she tried to peel his
hand away from her cheek.

He obliged by dropping his hand.

'What do you think you're doing?' she demanded
on a wave of new alarm as Richard slipped both
hands around her waist and pulled her to himself.
'Let me go! I don't like being. . .mauled,' she
snapped, struggling wildly.

Richard tightened his hold. 'Mauling is not what I have in mind, and "touched" was what you were going to say. Have you got a phobia about being touched, Julia?' he asked softly.

Only when touched by Richard Weldon because everything inside her seemed to go haywire and she felt as scared and threatened as he said she did, her pretences and defences useless against him—and herself.

Very deliberately, Richard spread his hands flat over the roundness of her buttocks, and she tried not to breathe because each agitated breath brought her hard against him. She stared at him helplessly, then gave an involuntary gasp as the pressure over her buttocks increased, while all the time he watched her through his lashes as if he was noting the reactions of the subject of some fascinating experiment.

When, finally, he released his hold, it was only to put his hands to her hair, unpinning it from its careless topknot to fall over her shoulders so he could lace his fingers through the soft, thick mass. Heart pounding, mouth dry, Julia just stood there.

'Darling Julia,' he murmured, his eyes holding her mesmerised while his fingers kept playing through her hair. 'So sophisticated, so sure of herself. . .so sure of where she thinks she wants to go, and, underneath it all, so soft and vulnerable.'

The tantalising fingers were no longer in her hair but peeling back the robe from her shoulders. She felt a tremor rock her at the touch of cool hands on warm bare skin, before Richard lowered his head into the curve of her neck, and then she knew she should stop him, and did try to make a protest, but found the words caught back in her throat. She closed her eyes, the stranger in her revelling in the long, throbbing kiss that had the effect of starting a little avalanche of alien, pulsating sensations deep inside her which just went on and on, gathering momentum as Richard's warm, moist mouth moved all along the length of one shoulder and slowly all the way back again before starting a new trail of kisses over her breast.

No man had ever touched—kissed—her breast. Shock vied with mounting excitement, and that with a surge of aroused pleasure as Richard's mouth reached its goal and closed over a hardened nipple. She drew in her breath in a small sharp gasp and raised her hands to his head—to push it away, she might have thought had she been capable of thought, but her fingers laced through his hair instead, holding him to her as she swayed mindlessly, making soft, whimpering sounds that she couldn't control.

The naked hunger in Richard's eyes when he finally brought his head up from her breast was something Julia had never seen in any man's eyes. And what did he see in her own as she flung her arms around his neck and drew his mouth down to her aching lips? She didn't care. With a shuddering sigh, she leaned into him as Richard wrapped his arms around her. There was an unsuppressed urgency in his hungrily probing mouth and in the hard, bruising body crushing against her; his carefully controlled seductive little game was over and he was no longer any more in control of his passion than she was.

Julia snapped her eyes open and blinked when he

suddenly tore his mouth away; the next moment, she felt the robe hauled roughly back over her shoulders. Richard's eyes were hard with a strange, glittering anger as he snatched up her hand and crushed her fingers around the closed fronts of the robe.

CHAPTER SEVEN

'I WON'T stay or you'll be accusing me of attaching strings to the managership after all,' Richard said bitterly through the smile that was a grimace, and Julia felt stunned, somehow cheated, but, most of all, rebuffed.

'I wasn't aware that I'd asked you to,' she rallied viciously after the dumbstruck pause in which she thought she would die of mortification.

'No? Then you'd better watch the body language, my sweet,' Richard retorted harshly, already moving away from her. 'See Rod in Branch Admin, first thing tomorrow morning; he'll tell you what's on the agenda,' he told her from the doorway, and might have switched to a foreign language she didn't understand. 'Don't bother to see me out.'

She could not have moved to see him out or if the house was on fire. 'Damn the managership, please stay!' Oh God, had she cried that out aloud? No, she couldn't have; Richard's hurried footsteps continued down the stairs without slowing, then the door slammed and he was gone. Julia stood staring unseeingly into space long after the Rover had growled out of the mews, finally coming back to life because she was shivering so violently her knees would have given way if she hadn't got herself on to the nearest chair in the dining alcove.

Relief. Gratitude that the managership was hers—

that was what had turned her head. Her career was still the most important thing, wasn't it? What else could it have been? Julia swung into instant rationalisation, winded by the force of the emotions that had nearly reduced her to begging Richard to stay and make love to her; that had nearly swept away her every principle. . .every warning her mother had drummed into her over long, bitter years. They would have all melted without a trace in Richard's arms if he hadn't stopped the lovemaking when he did, and she ought to be grateful to him for that. Ought to—only for the moment the feeling of rejection was too raw and painful to allow anything like gratitude or reason. She had wanted him, plain and simple, and, expert that she was, and try as she might, she could not rationalise that fact away, nor that Richard was the last man in the world she should have wanted for whatever reason.

Tarred with the same brush—the Nicholas Radcliffes and Richard Weldons. . .men who came strolling into women's lives demanding reaction. . . acknowledgement of their masculinity; demanding, and getting, response, then walking away when it suited them, leaving a trail of bitter memories, and sometimes something more tangible, behind them. An unwanted child, for instance. Dangerous men, and Julia had instinctively recognised Richard as one of the breed, and just as instinctively had gone on the defensive, instantly hostile and determined to think the worst of him. Mistresses. . .trading favours—not trusting his motives an inch. Not trusting herself, more like—and with reason, if tonight's emotional melt-down was any indication.

It was ages before Julia could get to sleep, and then only to drift in and out of uneasy dozes, between which she lay staring up at the ceiling, trying to fight the images that were like snatches from a film as her mind kept flinging her back into Richard's arms.

The reflection in the mirror next morning stared back at her with eyes opaque with tiredness, white skin drawn tightly over the high cheekbones, and a general air of having slept badly that not even spending twice as long over her make-up could counteract. She pulled her hair back into a severe knot at the nape because the style made her look more business-like and less a tired, unhappy little girl, and she needed all the help she could get to project the image of a manager in the making. She certainly didn't feel like one.

Deliberately arriving at the car park well past Richard's time of arrival really did bring home that she had been the one responsible for those weeks of coincidence which Richard had taken as encouragement—signals of some sort, but, heavens above, a man would have to be scraping to latch on to something so unintentional and so innocent. Or flattering himself. Yet when she had given the ultimate boost to his ego—shown herself available and willing— Richard had turned his back on her and walked away. Was that all he had wanted from her? An admission that she was as vulnerable and as attracted as his ego wished? And where did that leave her? With her well-ordered life disordered, confused, and not sure of anything any more when she should have been feeling on top of the world. . .the prized job hers, another career goal achieved, instead of which she was heading for the office with all the pleasure and excitement of going off to join the dole queue.

Most of the morning was spent upstairs in Branch Administration, going over the general plans for the Dawlish transformation into Weldons. There was no sign of Richard, and Julia didn't expect him to be at the meeting in the boardroom after lunch either, which was probably naïve of her, because if she'd thought about it she would have realised that Richard would need to be at the first official meeting. But she hadn't thought about it, and when she saw him sitting at the head of the long, polished table, she froze just inside the door.

Although she was vaguely conscious of other people in the room, there was nobody but Richard and herself as their eyes engaged in the timeless heart-stopping moment before Richard rose from his seat. One hand raised, he came towards her, and for a fleeting, mad second Julia thought he was about to take her into his arms right there in front of everybody, but the raised hand was only to beckon her into the room.

'Good afternoon, Julia.' The formal courtesy catapulted her back to earth and into the room with a thud.

'Good afternoon, Richard,' she returned, and must have sounded and looked quite normal, because nobody was staring at her as if she were mad.

'Let me introduce you to David Foster; he's the chap who's in the process of revamping Dawlish into shape. . .'

Richard led her around the room making further introductions, after which Julia took her seat, her self-possession restored a little by the formalities. As the meeting progressed, she found herself very much an integral part of it. . .asked for opinions, for her assessment of the Dawlish area, of local properties. The points she raised were listened to and discussed, and any other time it would have been heady stuff, being accepted as a competent professional by other competent professionals. Richard's doing—he had set the tone for the others to follow, and yet just by being in the room he took away the pleasure Julia might have felt in participating in her first management meeting proper. As it was, she had to concentrate madly to keep her mind on the matters at hand, and off the man at the top of the table who was formal, courteous, remote—the boss. And she was just another employee, and those wonderful, exciting moments in his arms last night might never have happened.

Richard left the meeting the moment it was over, setting the pattern for all the other meetings he attended, which wasn't all of them, so Julia could never tell when to expect him and could never really prepare herself for the impact of that first, long look down the polished table. And each time Richard acted as if nothing had ever happened between them. . .never sought her out for a private word afterwards, nor any other time during the days, and then weeks, that followed. It was courteous, friendly co-operation with a vengeance, and unbearable, although what it was she wanted from him Julia could not have put into words.

A resolution of unfinished business? Had they any unfinished business? She didn't know. But she did know she couldn't stand the way she felt in the wake of Richard's stand-off. . .the flatness that seemed to have engulfed her. . .the vague but persistent sense of hurt. . .her lack of concentration. How could she give her best to the most important job of her life when she felt as lacklustre as she had under that ass Jeremy's awful regime, the only merciful difference being that, here at Weldons, she was kept busy in spite of herself?

Personnel had given her carte blanche to hire whom she needed, other than the surveyor who was to come to her from another Weldons branch. Mr Matthaws had taken what Julia suspected had been a heavily gilded, if not actually golden, handshake, but she wanted Moira to accept the office administrator's job again, and had been trying to contact her friend for nearly two weeks before Moira finally telephoned in answer to the note Julia had resorted to sending her.

They arranged to meet for lunch at their customary venue just around the corner from Dawlish. Julia arrived first, settled at their usual table to wait for her friend, and then couldn't believe her eyes when Moira walked in, looking at least a stone lighter for starters, her greying hair shaped into a bouncing, youthful style, its greyness diluted with shimmering silver highlights, and face glowing and looking all of ten years younger.

A face-lift? Julia wondered, unable to take her eyes off her friend. 'Moira, you look wonderful!' she burst out after they had greeted each other with a kiss.

'Do I? Thank you. I feel wonderful,' Moira

laughed, delighted, as she settled into the seat
opposite Julia. Julia felt the blue eyes taking in her
own appearance and didn't miss the flicker of surprise. There was no way Moira, nor anyone else,
could tell her she looked wonderful without lying.
Moira chose not to lie. 'Well, how does it feel to be
manager of dear old Dawlish at last?' she asked
smilingly instead.

Julia shrugged. 'Fine, I suppose. Great,' she
amended when Moira lifted a newly defined eyebrow
at the first part of the unenthusiastic reply. 'I'm so
busy I don't know whether I'm coming or going half
the time,' Julia added with a laugh that must have
sounded as forced to Moira as it did to herself.
'Speaking of which,' she ran on quickly, 'you must
be coming and going at a great rate yourself lately.
I've tried for nearly two weeks to reach you.'

Moira nodded, smiling. 'I have been busy,' she
confessed with another cheerful laugh, and it struck
Julia that she had never seen her friend so happy.
'It's been wonderful,' Moira added cryptically. 'But,
darling, I did mean to ring you the moment I heard
the news. I'm ever so pleased for you, and I know
Richard couldn't have made a better appointment.'

Richard now, was it? 'Has he spoken to you—
about staying on at Dawlish—Weldons, I mean?'

'Hard to get used to it, isn't it?' Moira chuckled.
'I've just come past there now and it looks as if a
bomb has hit it! Yes, he has spoken to me, so don't
even think of trying to persuade me where your
lovely Richard tried and failed.'

'Lovely Richard?' Julia almost yelped. She stared at
Moira, amazed.

'I said no and I meant it,' Moira went on firmly. 'Though what I didn't tell him,' she leaned over the table, her voice suddenly half coy, half confidential, 'was that I had nicer plans for my future.'

'Go on,' Julia encouraged, intrigued, when Moira hesitated with what she could have sworn was a blush.

'Well, Cyril and I. . .we decided to use the closing of Dawlish as we both knew it to. . .to do other things,' Moira confided, proudly and reluctantly at the same time and not clarifying a thing.

'Cyril?' Julia repeated the name, mystified.

'Mr Matthews,' Moira enlightened her with an embarrassed little snap. 'We're getting married and moving to the country,' she added in a bite-the-bullet and get-it-over-with rush.

Julia managed, just, to hold back the incredulous shriek. 'Moira, that's terrific!' she broke into speech at last, flabbergasted, yes, but delighted for her friend—and 'Cyril', and tickled pink that there must have been a romance pottering along under her nose for years without her getting a hint of it.

'Don't say you're not stunned witless, because everybody else is—Cyril and myself included,' Moira giggled girlishly. 'But I'm only forty-eight, Julia, it's not that ancient,' she pointed out defensively. 'And Cyril is only fifty-seven. We've got years ahead of us and we'd really like to enjoy them doing something we've both wanted to do for a long time. We're planning to take over a general store in a small village in Dorset. Cyril's people come from there and that's where we've been for the last two weeks—seeing to things.'

'Sounds marvellous,' said Julia still weak with surprise, a strange pang of envy tugging at her.

'It will be a lot of hard work too, but it will be different—not like working for someone else in an office—you know what I mean. . .running your own show. . .having your own business. . .

'I know what you mean,' Julia said rather shortly.

'So you should, darling. Then why aren't you bubbling over with your dream job handed to you on a plate?' Moira suddenly asked point-blank. 'What's gone wrong, Julia?'

Julia stared at her friend bleakly, fighting the urge to confide, to drop the pretence and tell Moira she didn't know what had happened to her over the last two weeks since Richard had stormed out of her house and left her feeling he had pulled the rug from under her feet. 'Oh, I don't know. . .anticlimax, I suppose,' she equivocated, sheer stubborn pride preventing her from confessing that she had discovered what Moira had been trying to tell her for years: that a job couldn't be the be-all and end-all of anybody's existence, that now she wanted something more. 'I just seem to feel so tired all the time. . .washed out. Nothing to worry about; I'll be back in form in no time once Dawlish—Weldons, is open and——' 'I'm away from Richard,' she had nearly said. 'And I'm running my own show,' she managed to substitute in time. 'That's only a week and a half away now.' She brightened her voice, not very convincingly. 'There's going to be a branch launching party the Friday before it opens; you will come to that, won't you?'

'Yes, of course. Richard has mentioned it to me

already and I wouldn't miss it for the world.' Moira
allowed herself to be distracted from her curiosity, or
concern, about Julia. 'And since you've mentioned
parties, I hope you won't feel too tired to come
to. . .our evening on Saturday. I was going to telephone you about it.'

'Your. . .evening?' Julia frowned, perplexed.

'A sort of celebration. Cyril's sister insists.' Moira's
face turned a pretty shade of pink.

'An engagement party, you mean!' Julia grinned
wickedly, delighted at Moira not being able to own
up to having any such thing. Then her face fell.
'Moira, I can't!' she wailed. 'Nick is coming up to
London this weekend —you know, my cousin
Derek's son. We arranged it when I was there a
couple of weekends ago. I've promised to take him
to some dreadful film he's been dying to see on the
Saturday night, and then his friend's parents will
pick him up on Sunday morning and take him back
to Kent with them,' she elaborated, long-winded in
her nervousness that Moira might feel slighted.

'Never mind, you'll just have to come to the
wedding instead. There'll be no getting out of that,'
Moira laughed, not slighted at all.

'Just try and stop me,' Julia returned, and they
parted soon after, on that bright, jokey note, Julia
hurrying back to the office to run through the list of
some good employment agencies which might possibly be able to produce an experienced office administrator at virtually a moment's notice, and wishing
her friend had chosen a more convenient time to tie
the knot. Churlish thought. Julia cancelled it instantly
and mentally beamed a contrite apology to Moira.

Employment agencies rung, appointments made, and a half-hour session with Personnel over, Julia was heading back to her desk after a detour via the development department to pick up a file she wanted, when Eleanor waylaid her outside the lifts.

The senior woman could not have been more pleasant or helpful since their crossed wires about managerships had untangled themselves. 'Message for you on your desk, Julia. Richard wants you to ring him. You are being kept busy, aren't you?' Eleanor's laugh carried a slight edge of friendly envy. 'So shall I be soon, and I wish to goodness Cliff would hurry up and take himself off so I can make a start. He and Richard have just returned from two days' reconnaissance in Scotland, and Richard is going back there next week, so it does look as if things are about to move at long last, although I suppose they're waiting for your Dawlish to be out of the way before they really get going on Scotland,' Eleanor went on, incidentally explaining Richard's absence from the office the last few days.

Julia could barely listen; the mere mention of Richard's name these days seemed to make her seize up inside. She murmured some hasty, distracted responses which she hoped made sense, and escaped Eleanor's chatter in a sea of turmoil.

What could Richard want to talk to her about after two weeks of avoiding her? Business or. . .? Business; it could only be business. Julia poured cold water on the faint spark of hope that it might be something else. Then why hadn't he given Eleanor the message to pass on? Because Eleanor was no longer her supervisor, the chain of management now being direct from Richard to herself, that was why, Julia reasoned dully, tipping more water on the recalcitrant spark as she reached for the telephone, then nearly jumped out of her skin when it started ringing before she put her hand on it. She was going to have to do something about those nerves, but soon. She picked up the instrument on the third ring.

'Julia Radcliffe,' she said with an effort to sound businesslike.

'Richard. Didn't you get my message?' The first words he had spoken to her in weeks without half a dozen people around, and there was no 'hello, Julia,' no 'how are you?' The spark of hope that he too might have wanted to resolve the nerve-shredding status quo between them vanished at last, and served her right for being so silly.

'I've only just got back to my desk this moment,' Julia returned, sharp in her disappointment. 'I was with Personnel and then I dropped in on Development to pick up the plans of that conversion behind Notting Hill Gate. . .' She stopped and heard nothing but silence. 'You know—Hetherington House. There's a point I wanted to query. . .something I feel ought to be changed in the plans.' She talked on just to keep talking. 'Can I do that? Make suggestions? You see, I——' she stopped again. 'Richard. . .?'

'Still here,' he informed her tersely. 'Although, frankly, I wonder if you'd have noticed if I weren't.'

Julia flushed. 'I'm not in the habit of talking to myself,' she muttered. 'How was your trip to Scotland?'

Richard growled an unamused laugh. 'Don't go

overboard with the civilities. It was fine.' He dismissed her effort at pleasantry with stinging offhandedness. 'How has it been going at your end? Hired your staff yet? What about Moira? Talked to her?'

Business. Nothing but business. Julia winced and could only be glad he couldn't see the disappointment written all over her face. 'Yes, we had lunch today, as a matter of fact. She's not interested, as she had apparently told you, and you'd have saved me a lot of time and trouble if you'd bothered to tell me you had already spoken to her.' Julia rallied a little with the snap. 'I've been on to some agencies, though, and they'll be sending people in for interviews next week. I've already been interviewing for the two negotiators and secretary and I think I——'

'That should keep you happy,' Richard cut her off tartly.

'Busy,' Julia corrected him sharply.

'Then you should be in your element.'

Yes, damn it, she should be. And the reason she wasn't was on the other end of the line sniping at her. She didn't want to talk to him any more—about anything. 'Is that it, Richard? Anything else you want to know?' she asked, all at once very brisk.

'Actually, yes. I wondered what you were doing on Saturday evening,' he muttered, and Julia wondered whether her ears were playing tricks on her. 'I thought we might get together and discuss more properties,' he added, and if it was meant to be a joke it fell awfully flat; he sounded gauche and surly, but he was asking her out for all that. Julia's heart began skipping furiously.

And then she remembered Nick, and it was just

like that other time when Richard had invited her to lunch and fate had intervened in the form of Andrew Reith. This time, however, she wasn't going to fall into the trap of fibbing. 'I'm afraid I've already made arrangements for Saturday evening,' she started carefully, and didn't get any further.

'With Reith, I suppose,' Richard jumped in with his wrong conclusion. 'I'll see you around.' He hung up on her just like that, without giving her a chance to explain about Nick, or tell him she did want to go out with him another evening, any other evening. . .any other day, but Saturday.

Damn it, she was going to tell him and he was going to listen! Her hand reached to the telephone, hovered in a moment's uncertainty—just long enough for pride to return, or was it fear that she might put her foot in it trying to explain about Nick. . .be reduced to feeble lies and make things worse between them? And would Richard believe that it was only a fourteen-year-old boy she was putting up for the night?

Or would have put up if he had turned up. In another back-hander from the fates, Nick's mother telephoned on Friday evening to say Nick wouldn't be coming after all because he had sprained his ankle playing football that afternoon. Ankle or wrist? Julia couldn't remember, and what difference did it make? The damage was done; she had put Richard off for nothing.

It did mean that she could go to Moira's 'evening', though; Julia toyed with that option off and on all day Saturday and decided she couldn't face it; she was not in the mood for other people's happiness, and she spent a miserable, solitary Saturday evening watching television and fighting the urge to telephone Richard and tell him her previous engagement had fallen through and suggesting he come over and. . .what?

What would he take that to mean? That she was available? Well, wasn't she? Ready and willing and available to plunge into an affair, if that was what Richard wanted. Was she mad? Probably; there was no other explanation for her obsessive thoughts. . .for Richard on her mind day and night like a headache that wouldn't go away. Was the attraction sex or love? Julia had spent her adult life avoiding sex and anything remotely resembling love, never loved or been loved, so how could she tell now what it was she felt? Or why. And did it matter, anyway?

She telephoned Richard's house at nine-thirty. He was ex-directory, but all his staff had his private number, only Julia had never envisaged a time she would want to use it—need to telephone Richard Weldon on a Saturday night to say 'Come over and I think I'm in love with you.'

Would she have really said that? She never found out. A woman's voice answered Richard's telephone, and Julia flung down the phone at her end as if it had turned live and bitten her.

CHAPTER EIGHT

A HOUSEKEEPER. Men like Richard had house-keepers, didn't they? Maybe they did, but they also had girlfriends—mistresses. In mews houses, no less.

The scenario Julia had dismissed as part of her earlier self-defensive hostility towards him now reared in her mind again, accompanied by all the bells and whistles of jealousy in top form. Hurt, resentment and consuming red-hot anger whirled and warred furiously before eventually churning down into a dull relief that Richard himself hadn't answered the phone because there was no saying what sort of idiot she might have made of herself. Besides, she began to reason as the trickle of ration-alisation gathered momentum, the woman could well have been Richard's mother, sister, aunt, cousin— even grandmother, for that matter.

'But not wife!' Julia finished the inventory of Richard's possible female relatives with a triumphant little laugh. Not wife, because one of the very few personal things she did know about him was that he did not have a wife. He was not the marrying kind. And that made two of them.

In the morning, it was as if a fever had broken and the madness passed; Julia felt rational, in control, but with an odd undercurrent of energy that wouldn't allow her to sit still for a moment, the by-product a thoroughly spring-cleaned house which she didn't want to stay in.

On impulse, she took herself out for lunch at one of the eateries in the high street and lingered to mingle among the springtime tourists wandering about, deep down afraid that, if she was alone and undistracted, the craziness of the previous evening might strike again and goad her into doing something she could regret more than the abortive telephone call. Going to Richard's house, for instance.

It was going on three when she turned the corner of her mews and saw the green Rover parked at her door, Richard standing beside it. Turn around and flee back up the high street or run and hurl herself into his arms? Julia couldn't tell which thought came first, but she acted on neither; she made herself walk on slowly, conscious of Richard watching her approach—impassively, as he might have a stranger's.

'I've brought over the keys to Hetherington House,' he said casually as she drew up to him, and it took her a good few seconds to work out what Hetherington House was, let alone when she had spoken to him about it, and then she stared at him in blank disbelief.

'You said you were interested in it, so I thought you'd want to look it over,' Richard explained testily, as if he had put himself out at her request—or something.

He had come over just to take her on a tour of inspection of some Weldons property? Apparently.

'Now?' Julia asked, bewildered, and not wanting to believe that it was only business that had brought him here. Was that what he'd had in mind for their 'date' last night? Hetherington House by candlelight?

'If you're not busy.' He sounded as if he grudged giving her the loophole.

'I. . . No, I'm not busy.'

'Then we can set off.' He gestured at the car parked against her garage door.

Julia studied the Rover as if she had never seen one before, then brought her eyes back to Richard. 'Yes, why not?' she suddenly trilled gaily, and added a flash of teeth in a brilliant smile. Why not, indeed? A tour of a clapped-out old building was the best offer she had had all day—and the only offer she was ever going to get from Richard. That was what he was telling her in his not very subtle way, wasn't it? That business was the only thing between them, and she should have realised that from his behaviour towards her the last two weeks. He was not interested in her any more. It hurt; it stung, but by golly, Richard Weldon was never going to know that. 'I've simply been dying to inspect the place ever since I saw the conversion plans,' Julia trilled again as she tossed the navy jacket she'd been carrying over the back of the passenger seat and climbed in beside him.

'So I gathered,' he muttered sourly, and gave one of those abrupt, angry laughs she couldn't quite fathom, but hated.

'I mean, it's so interesting to see a place in its original condition first, isn't it? Before the conversion gets under way.' Julia plunged into determined prattle and went on and on. . .about how interested she was in the redevelopment of down-at-the-heel areas. . .how the face of London seemed to be changing before her very eyes. . . The fatuous commentary kept rolling off her tongue—decidedly one-sided commentary. Richard drove in dead silence, tension radiating from him in almost physical blasts and Julia half expected him to burst out with a 'for God's sake, shut up!' and wished she could. She was starting to repeat herself, regurgitating the same nauseous phrases, and in the end she stopped in mid-sentence, unable to stand the sound of her own voice a moment longer. She stared dismally out of the side window at the scaffolding in front of every second building they passed—reinforcing at least some of her mindless comments about areas ripe for redevelopment.

'Did you have a nice evening yesterday?'

Given the state of her nerves, the apropos-of-nothing question which seemed squeezed through Richard's teeth, it wasn't surprising Julia didn't know what he was talking about. 'Yesterday?' she repeated, turning to him with a frown. 'Oh, you mean last night with Nick? No, he sprained his ankle and couldn't come.'

'Nick?' Richard took his eyes off the road for an instant to give her a brief, surprised glance. 'I thought Reith's name was Andrew.'

'It is. Nick is my cousin's son. He's fourteen years old and was coming for the weekend so I could take him to a film,' Julia said, very tightly, and wondered why she bothered to explain—justify herself. It was not Richard's business who she was or wasn't with, any more than it was hers as to who he was entertaining last night.

'Too bad,' he said carelessly. 'Here we are,' he added, pulling into the kerb.

The building was grim grey and gloomy, with decades of neglect giving a haunted-house look to its shabby Victorian façade. There had been a photograph of it in the file, along with the developer's artistic presentation of an 'after' picture. If one looked at the actual building, it was hard not to conclude that someone had gone wild on the imagination, yet Julia knew that in six months' time the 'before' would match the 'after' and, in real estate parlance, be 'a very desirable property' indeed.

They went up the steps between the fat, peeling columns and Richard unlocked the door and led the way into the dingy, musty hall, still with its dirty, threadbare carpet, paintwork peeling and wallpaper coming off the damp walls in shreds. An unprepossessing sight if ever there was one.

'Welcome to your first big brief,' Richard quipped with a grim laugh. 'Appalling, isn't it?'

'For the moment,' answered Julia, defensive of 'her property' and went on ahead to inspect it—which was what he had brought her for. She poked her nose into all the rooms on the ground floor first, then trailed down into the basement, and back up to climb the filthy, but quite safe, staircase, all the way to the attics. Six floors in all, counting the basement and the attics, and almost every room had been a bedsitter in its day, with only the odd, unexpected one-bedroom flat turning up on a couple of the upper floors.

In spite of herself, the bleakness of her mood and of the surroundings, she felt a stir of interest—more

than that: a faint but unmistakable sense of excitement. 'Her property'. Her first big brief. In her
mind's eye, the transformation was complete; she
could picture the garden flats, duplex apartments,
light, airy top-floor flats—all costing a small fortune,
yet quite reasonable in terms of current prices, and
an absolute steal in comparison to some of the
Dockland conversions.

Richard had stayed downstairs; she found him in
one of the back rooms on the ground floor, staring
out through the grime-encrusted window. 'Well?' he
said, turning to her as she came in.

'Great,' she replied with enthusiasm—the genuine, unfeigned enthusiasm she thought had deserted
her forever. Not so, it seemed, and if she could
resurrect a little more of it she might manage to get
the job, herself, and Richard, back into perspective
yet. She joined him at the window and surveyed the
small, scraggy plot of ground that would soon be
landscaped into the handkerchief-sized gardens of
what, in erstwhile parlance, used to be the basement
flats.

'What was it you thought needed changing in the
plans?' asked Richard, surprising her that he remembered her comment from their last testy telephone
conversation. Did he commit every word she uttered
to memory?

Julia hesitated. 'Would they take any notice of
someone like me? The developers, I mean? I know
they've got their architects and—well. . .' she
shrugged '. . .I'm only a negotiator.'

'Branch manager, surely,' he corrected suavely.
'And yes, they'll take notice if it suits them, and if

they stand to make more money, then they'll take a very gratifying lot of notice,' he assured her drily.

'Well. . .' Julia began again reluctantly. 'It's just that upstairs—right up there in the attic part—instead of having two two-bedroom flats, wouldn't it be better to have three one-bedrooms, or even two one-bedrooms and two little studio flats?'

'Why?' Richard queried with a sharpness that made her feel she was presenting a case in the boardroom.

'Well, economically speaking, it would bring in a higher profit for the floor.' Very deliberately, she made the point about money first. 'But, aside from that, it would also make the flats more affordable.'

'For whom?'

'For people who can't afford two-bedroom flats, obviously,' she returned, more snappishly than she intended.

'Such as?' Richard persisted, looking at her curiously.

'Such as single women,' Julia came out with the punchline at last, and wished she had just presented the money angle and left it at that.

The sudden grin lit up his face in a way she had not seen for ages. 'What did you have in mind up there? A cloister or a feminist stronghold?' he asked teasingly, and another time, another place, she might have responded to the quip in like vein, glad to use it as a bridge across the tension between them. Right at the moment, though, she could not even raise a smile.

'Forget I mentioned it,' she muttered, embarrassed and angry with herself. 'We'd better go now, don't you think?' She was already charging across the room and had reached the front door before Richard caught up with her.

'It was just a mild joke, Julia, for heaven's sake! Don't get up in arms about it.'

'I'm not,' she retorted, leaving him to lock up and almost running down the steps and to the car. An irrational over-reaction to a mild joke. How could Richard have known his innocent quip would hit such a vulnerable spot? He hadn't meant to make fun of her concern for women like herself who needed the security and independence that owning the roof over their heads could bring.

He gave her a long, silent look as he handed her into the car and stayed silent for most of the drive. Julia was conscious of the brief glances at her stony profile, but refused to meet his eye. Still locked in prickly embarrassment, she preferred the silence to any attempt at small talk.

'Did you have a hard time buying your place?'

Small talk, or did he really want to know?

'Did you?' Richard was not about to be put off by her discouraging lack of response.

Julia shrugged sullenly. 'I was in a better position than most women my age because my mother left me what she'd managed to save before she died, so I had a reasonable deposit towards the first place I bought,' she told him grudgingly, without turning to look at him, and resenting that she felt compelled to tell him anything at all when a simple 'yes' or 'no' would have sufficed. And then she couldn't leave it alone. 'Not everybody is so lucky—my mother never was. She had to rely on my father to provide a roof over her head, and then work at menial jobs she hated to support me after he dumped us at the earliest opportunity.' Usually suppressed, the bitterness came through shockingly and, too late, Julia regretted every angry word of her disclosure.

'So that's it!' Richard murmured softly as if something had become clear to him, when he could not have had a clue. She could guess what he had concluded—that she was some sort of shrewish feminist as well as a single-minded career woman.

'No, it's not!' she shot back hotly. 'And you've no right to make assumptions about me.'

His drawn-out sigh was a hiss of frustration. 'Maybe I haven't,' he admitted testily, 'only you make it so damned hard not to when you barricade yourself behind your six-foot wall and won't let anyone reach you.'

It was a lot safer behind the barricade; you knew exactly where you were. Venture out from behind it, and it was all unfamiliar territory. . .a dangerous minefield of emotions she had never come across before. . .of confusing situations she didn't know how to handle. The trouble was, Julia doubted if she was ever going to be able to retreat behind her wall again, not entirely.

The Rover was bumping gently over the cobblestones of her mews. This, at least, was familiar territory; she breathed a mental sigh of relief to be home again. Hand in position on the door-handle for a quick get away, she turned to him as he pulled up outside her house and switched off the engine. 'Thank you for taking me to view Hetherington House,' she said with stiff formality. 'I apprec——'

The stilted vote of thanks came to an abrupt end as Richard suddenly leaned over her and snatched her hand off the door.

'What the hell else could I do to get you to spend some time with me?' he demanded savagely, his face close and contorted into jagged anger. 'That's right, a ploy,' he rasped bitterly in answer to the blank surprise on her face. 'Typical—that's what you're thinking now, isn't it? Underhand. . .devious; yes, I'm exactly as you'd told yourself I was.' He dropped her hand into her lap with a self-disgusted fling. 'Well, while you're at it, Julia, you can add more deviousness to your catalogue—to wit, all those meetings I turned up to for weeks that I didn't need to be at. I came so I could sit there and watch you being all businesslike and efficient and all the while thinking of how beautiful you looked when I started making love to you that Sunday night. Did you realise that? No, of course you didn't. You acted as if I didn't exist. Yes, it is funny, isn't it?' He nodded, as Julia broke into an involuntary shocked laugh.

She shook her head dumbly; it was not funny and she wasn't laughing at him, only at the absurd irony of sitting through those self-same meetings, unable to concentrate because her mind was on Richard, ice-polite and remote at the head of the table, and not daring to look at him for fear she would give her own miserable thoughts away. While all the time. . .? How could two grown people be so mixed up. . .as insecure as teenagers with their first infatuations? Herself, yes; she was just about on par with today's teenagers, but Richard? Confident. Arrogant. Was he? The man beside her looked so vulnerable Julia had to fight the urge to wrap her arms around him and tell him it was OK; she was as crazy as he was.

'Not funny, pathetic.' Richard twisted out a weary smile. 'But God, Julia, I want you, and if that means I've got to take a back seat to your career, all right, I'll take a back seat and. . .' The expression on his face changed, softening into uncertainty, while his eyes combed her face with a reluctant hope. 'Julia, if you keep looking at me like that I'll. . .'

'You'll what. . .?' she heard herself whisper huskily, putting a hand to his cheek and stroking it gently. Then while Richard stared back, seemingly mesmerised by her action, she curved the hand around the back of his head and drew it down for the kiss that, for her, was an explosion of the longing that had been tormenting her since she was last in his arms. She was conscious of his hesitancy. . .of an unsureness in him—as if he didn't quite trust her not to pull away, before he finally responded to her pleading mouth with a force that almost winded her.

In the end, she had to drag her mouth away just so she could draw breath.

'I want you,' Richard said jaggedly, leaning over her so that she had to stay reclining against the back of the seat.

'Yes.' Yes, he wanted her; yes, she wanted him— and nothing else from him. . .no commitment, no guarantee of a future with him. She looked back unwaveringly into his dark, uncertain eyes. Didn't he understand what she was trying to tell him with that one little word? The 'yes' covered everything she was too afraid to explain because whatever they said to each other had a way of foundering in a sea of misinterpretation. 'Would you like to come up for coffee?' Julia startled them both with the trite, traditional invitation and felt gauche and nervous, and way out of her depth already. What *did* people say to each other after saying something as shattering as 'I want you'?

Richard nodded abruptly. 'OK,' he said brusquely, and seemed embarrassed as he moved off her to shift back into his seat. Julia straightened up and ran her fingers through her mussed-up hair, all at once aware of time and place, and hoping a neighbour hadn't been passing by.

'Hop out and I'll park the car against the garage,' Richard ordered with a casualness that might or might not have been genuine.

Coffee. All she had done was to invite him for a cup of coffee, she told herself as she watched him manoeuvre the Rover so it was flush against the garage door and leaving enough room for passing cars. She felt chilled because it was late afternoon and the air had turned nippy, that was all; and she felt scared out of her wits because. . .?

She broke into mad prattle about Hetherington House as Richard joined her, continued it as she let them in and kept up the breathless-voiced flow all the way up the stairs. At the top landing she flapped an agitated hand towards the sitting-room. 'Do go in. I'll just go and take off my jacket and be out to make coffee in a moment.'

'Forget the coffee.' He opened the bedroom door. Julia couldn't move. 'Don't say anything, Julia,' he ordered—pleaded—as she opened her mouth to make some sort of knee-jerk protest. 'Please don't say anything unless it's to tell me you want me. You do, don't you?' he demanded, a note of desperation in his voice. 'I haven't got it all wrong. . . I haven't gone mad, have I? In the car when you kissed me, you were telling me that you want me. . .want to make love with me?'

Keeping truth at bay was almost second nature to her these days; Julia could feel the pressure to run away from it just one more time—to lie to him. . .hurt him—anything to send him storming off so that she didn't give in to her own frightening need of him.

'Yes, I want you,' she told him in a barely audible whisper, and the next moment was in his arms, her own arms around his neck and their mouths locked, surrender. . .possession, all one. It was like straw going up in flames.

Richard looked dazed when he pulled his mouth away, wonder in his eyes, not the triumph Julia was half afraid would be in them as he slid her jacket off and tossed it at the chair in front of the dressing-table, returning his hands to her blouse to work on its buttons while he covered her face with kisses. Eyes, nose, cheeks, chin; the kisses rained everywhere before he took her mouth again to savour it with a slow, deep sensuousness that made Julia feel she was drowning in sweetness while at the same time hurting quite physically from the fiery longing low and deep inside her.

It took an age for Richard to undress her. . .an age punctuated by those long, sensuous kisses, by possessive hands lingering over her breasts as he removed their lacy covering. . .lingering over her hips as he drew the skirt down over them. . .lingering everywhere he touched and setting off tremors of excitement Julia couldn't control. She sensed the growing urgency in him, saw it glowing in his eyes as he flung himself out of his own clothes—in mere seconds, and then Julia, who had never seen a naked man in her life, other than in films, experienced a moment of irrational but very real panic. And yet instinctively she moved to him to be gathered into his arms, and the panic vanished at the contact of bare body against bare body, in its place a surge of arousal that brought out an involuntary gasp of shocked pleasure—or pleasurable shock—and a new set of sensations no words could have described.

Using his body as a guide, Richard was manoeuvring her across the room to the bed, releasing her to sweep back the covers and then easing her down—so carefully, she might have been made of porcelain. Propping himself up on an elbow, he lay beside her, looking and loving and already possessing her with his eyes.

'Richard. . .' It was a plea for his mouth. . .for his hands. For everything Julia had never experienced before and wanted desperately to experience with him now. She reached to him, touching caressingly. . .tentatively at first, then with increasing confidence and a little flare of triumph, as Richard bent over her on a groan of tortured ecstasy, his hands and mouth hers at last.

'Darling, I've been going crazy wanting you. I've wanted you from the moment I saw you,' he told her between the urgent kisses down her throat. 'Why

have you fought me so long? Why have we waited
so long for this?'

Her throat arching to his mouth and her body
undulating languidly under his stroking hand, Julia
was too consumed by her own delight to want to
talk. Did it matter any more why she had fought
him? Why they had waited so long for something
that, deep down, she had known was destined to
happen whether she fought against it or not.

'Why?' The low growl was warm and moist in her
ear. 'Why, darling? Why?' Richard persisted as if it
was important for him to know, when it wasn't
important at all. 'We could have been together weeks
ago.' He drew back to look at her reproachfully.

Eyes heavy lidded and half closed, Julia gazed back
through a dreamy mist of pleasure. 'I was scared,'
she said simply, and felt his hand stop dead in its
track along her thigh.

'Scared?' He mouthed the word frowningly, and
then she saw comprehension dawning in the puzzled
depths of his eyes. 'You've never done this before!'
he exclaimed thickly. 'Darling, I never guessed.' He
was shaking his head, frowning, and looking somehow angry with himself.

'No,' Julia murmured, not really in answer to his
statement. No, she had never done 'this' before; she
was a virgin, but not because she had been scared of
the physical act of sex as Richard thought; she had
been scared of the emotional involvement which
might follow willy-nilly, or a need for a commitment
she knew she could never expect from any man.
Scared of everything, in fact, only she couldn't
explain all that to Richard, least of all now, when

nothing really mattered except her need of him. 'I want you.' She moved her hand down his body, trying to tell him how very much she did want him, and experienced a repeat of the little flare of feminine triumph as his expression changed and his body responded to her caresses.

'Darling, darling Julia,' he murmured, burrowing his face into her neck.

There was a new gentleness in his hands and in his mouth as they resumed their erotic journey over her body, the tenderness more arousing than any savage passion. Julia arched and tossed uncontrollably, the aching need inside her intensifying inexorably with each stage of Richard's tour of discovery of her body. . .from the tips of her hardened nipples, over the swollen mounds of her breasts and downwards to secret places no man had ever touched before. She cried out as he drew up to cover her with his body, digging her fingers savagely into his shoulders and crying out again when he entered her, the spasms of pain and pleasure indistinguishable. 'Darling. Darling,' Richard poured the words into her mouth, hushing her cries with the engulfing kiss.

Timeless moments later, Julia flickered her eyes open and stared wonderingly into his as she began to move against him, her body telling him what she couldn't put into words and creating a rhythm to a beat of its own which Richard seemed to know too, and she thought she would go mad as the pleasure that was pure anguish welled and welled; yet she would have died if it stopped.

Nothing had prepared her for the final piercing peak; she felt rocked by an explosion that shattered her body and her mind; a white blaze of light flared behind her closed lids, and she was only dimly aware of Richard's hoarse cry as he abandoned his control at last and gave in to his own need of her.

Wrapped in his arms again, drained and blissfully content, Julia marvelled dazedly that two bodies could give such joy to each other—as if they had been made and brought together for that sole purpose.

'Darling. . .?' Richard's voice broke through a warm, fuzzy haze.

'Hmm?'

'Are you all right?'

'Wonderful.' She snuggled closer into him and felt the touch of his lips on her hair.

'Don't let me fall asleep, will you? I've a plane to catch to Scotland this evening.'

'Hmm,' she murmured drowsily, drifting unresistingly into a delicious doze, and when she surfaced to consciousness again she was alone.

Disconcerted, she sat up. It was dark outside, but the lamp on the bedside table was on; Richard must have switched it on before he left. Why hadn't he wakened her? Why had he just left like that, as if. . .? As if that was all there was to lovemaking—the wonderful, mind-blowing physical act, and not even a shared cup of coffee afterwards. Was that all he wanted from her—her body? Julia fought back the hurt and the doubts and regrets poised to spring forward with the next thought. And then she saw the envelope propped against the base of the lamp.

'I love you. See you Friday.'

She stared at the words Richard had scrawled on

the back of the envelope and felt a sweep of hope so fierce, it hurt. Richard loved her. Or did he gallantly leave the same message for all the women he took to bed? He had not said it to her once during his lovemaking. 'I want you', not 'I love you' had been the cry wrenched out from the depths of him in those last moments of passion. But they had been lover's eyes that had adored her body. . .lover's hands that had caressed her into a torment of ecstasy, and a lover's body had claimed her, and if that was only 'wanting' then she would accept it, and gladly, for however long Richard 'wanted'—weeks, months, it made no difference. She wanted him too. Loved him? Julia was too afraid to want to know. Perhaps later, when she felt more sure of him. . .of herself, she would face the question whether she loved Richard Weldon. Not yet. She didn't want to think about that now, nor about anything else that might intrude on the dizzying exhilaration of just being alive. . .happy, and counting the days until Richard returned from Scotland on Friday.

Julia wasn't expecting the telephone call the next evening. She had just returned from work having floated through a day of interviews and meetings with her feet scarcely touching the ground.

'Richard!' she breathed in surprise and delight, and tingling all over at the sound of his voice in her ear. 'I didn't expect to hear from you,' she ran on breathlessly. 'Did you catch your plane all right?'

'Just!' He laughed.

'You should have woken me,' she said reproachfully.

'Then I'd never have caught the plane, darling.

You were so beautiful I can't stop thinking about you for a moment.' The voice dropped to a husky purr and it was like being caressed all over again. 'Did you see my note?'

'Yes,' Julia murmured. 'Thank you,' she added like a good little girl remembering her manners.

Richard chuckled softly. 'That's not the answer you're supposed to give, but I can wait. You're going to have to tell me sooner or later that you love me too, you know.'

She caught back her breath and couldn't say anything for the sudden dryness in her mouth.

'I'll telephone again tomorrow,' Richard promised as he rang off, and he did. The evening after that too, and each call was the same. . .telling her he missed her, that she was beautiful and he couldn't wait to make love to her again.

Monday. Tuesday. Wednesday. Julia counted off the days after each call. One more day; one more call, and Richard would be back. On Friday evening he would be there in person at her door to take her to the Dawlish opening party. And bringing her home again. He had told her she was beautiful, but Julia was determined she was going to be even more beautiful for him that night.

'Oh, the trusty old black—that sort of thing,' Eleanor informed her with a dismissive laugh when Julia asked what the women wore to branch opening parties. 'Some of the chaps come straight from work, so don't bother dressing up. It's only a business do.'

For some people maybe. Julia went off during her lunch-hour on Thursday and bought a white velvet dress. It was absolutely gorgeous, outrageously expensive and, quite possibly, utterly unsuitable. Richard would love it, and Julia felt on top of the world.

CHAPTER NINE

WHAT made her take the short cut down Chiswell Mews? It wasn't even a short cut as such, only a means of bypassing the main road and its heavy, home-bound traffic for a block or so, and in all the time she had lived in her mews Julia had never thought of using the route either to or fro work.

So why now? she wondered as she cruised over the cobblestones, slowly, because there was no other way over cobblestones, and no way the woman coming out of the garage could have missed her as she drew alongside the house Richard had bought.

'Julia!' The tall, dark woman waved smilingly, and, short of ramming her foot on the accelerator and staging a mortifying getaway, there was nothing Julia could do but stop, her eyes glancing past the woman to the open garage and the green Rover inside it.

The sight of the car didn't shock her so much as the connection between 'the woman from Personnel' and the house in Chiswell Mews. And how had it escaped her so long? They had waved 'hellos' at each other at Weldons, chatted even, and, in spite of the thumping clue of Richard almost always being in the wings when this woman was around, Julia still hadn't twigged. It was a little like bumping into your bank manager on the beach—the face is familiar, but out of context, hard to place. Now, as she saw the woman in context, in the environment they had first met, all the pennies dropped like hailstones from the sky. Clare Risely. Widow from Norfolk. Looking for a base in London. The woman Richard had bought the house for.

'Hello, Clare,' Julia said through a glazed smile, and was amazed she could speak. 'Moved in already?'

Clare Risely bent to the window. 'Not quite. I'm only here to get the renovations moving along. The owner just moved out the other day after completion was rushed through. You remember? He wanted everything finalised as quickly as possible?'

'Yes.' Julia remembered telling her that when Clare came to view the house about a week or so before Richard. She also remembered Clare saying that someone else was involved in any purchase she made and would need to come to view the property before she could make a final decision. Richard.

'Would you like to come up for a coffee? Instant, I'm afraid. Do—if you're not in a hurry to get home,' Clare put in persuasively as Julia hesitated.

'No, I'm not in a hurry, and yes, thank you; I'd like a coffee.' Julia surprised herself with the acceptance.

She was not in any hurry any more; the anxiousness to be home for Richard's telephone call was gone, but nothing much else in its place—yet, except for a deadly flat calm and a strangely intense curiosity about Richard's mistress, real and alive in front of her eyes and never again to be dismissed as a figment of jealous imagination.

They went in through the garage.

'Richard left me his car on Sunday evening and

caught a taxi to Heathrow,' Clare volunteered as they skirted the Rover to get to the side door into the hall, and Julia felt her stomach given a sudden, uncontrollable heave, then felt a spasm of surprise that Clare took it for granted she knew of the connection between herself and Richard. It must be common knowledge around Weldons, and, malicious irony, Julia the only one not privy to it—an omission well and truly rectified now. 'It's been a boon for the running around I've needed to do, but I'll be bringing my own car down when I'm settled in, of course,' Clare added chattily.

'Of course,' Julia repeated weakly like an unwell parrot.

'Well, what do you think? Better already, isn't it?' Clare's gesture encompassed the tiny hall—minus its gilt mirror and the chandelier extravaganza.

'Oh, great,' Julia enthused mechanically, and wanted to turn and run. . .run away from this nice, friendly woman who had no idea what was going on—that Richard had betrayed her. As much as he had betrayed Julia. Had he really gone back to his mistress straight after making love to her on Sunday afternoon? Julia fought the urge to run, another assault of nausea on her stomach, and followed Clare up the stairs, concentrating on the cut of Clare's beautiful pale suede suit and trying not to think.

'Sorry there's nothing to sit on, but I do have two cups,' Clare apologised with a laugh as they entered the sitting-room, which didn't have a skerrick of furniture in it.

'Where are you staying now?' Julia asked abruptly, knowing the answer full well, but wanting to hear it from Clare's lips. Why? So she could feel even more sickened?

Clare gave her an odd look. 'Why, Richard's,' she confirmed, the faint surprise a reinforcement of her assumption that Julia was *au fait* with the relationship. 'I've been staying with him on and off for weeks while all this was being settled, but it won't be long now, I hope, before I can set up in here and get out of his hair. I rather think I cramp his style!' Clare tinkled out a laugh as she went behind the counter into the kitchenette.

Cramp that double-crossing rotter's style? Lady, have I got news for you! Julia left the vicious retort unvoiced and smiled tightly instead.

'It does have potential, doesn't it?' Clare was studying the empty room from behind the counter as she flicked the kettle on. 'Just wait until the painters and carpet people have done their work, you won't know the place. It is a bit small, unfortunately,' she frowned, measuring the room with her eyes, 'but if things work out for me, I'll be opening an office soon. Interior design,' she clarified as Julia looked blank, and then embarrassed that she hadn't remembered. 'Don't apologise,' Clare smiled. 'You can't possibly be expected to remember everything about every client you meet. Anyway, I'm planning to set up my own business, which is why I needed a London base, although I'd never have managed it at this stage without Richard's backing. He's been absolutely marvellous, and it's meant I didn't need to sell up my house in Norfolk.'

The nausea had left off to give way to the cold, hard knot tightening in her chest. Julia listened to

Clare chatter on while they sipped their coffees. About the sixteen-year-old twins at boarding school. . .about her life in Norfolk. . .about her plans for the business, and every second sentence had Richard in it—how good he was with the children, how wonderful he had been since Clare's husband had died four years ago. Julia was afraid she might scream.

The affair must be of at least four years' standing. . . Richard stepping in when the husband died— if not before. A comfortable, domestic sort of affair it sounded like, with the odd affair on the side as a break from routine—for Richard. Did Clare know? Guess? Was she too grateful to him to care? For a moment, Julia was tempted to divulge all about precious Richard. And what would that achieve? Nothing, if Clare already knew or suspected, and a cruel shattering of illusions if she didn't. It would be a spiteful thing to do. Julia made non-committal noises, finished her coffee and tried not to rush out of the house.

'Now that we're almost neighbours, I hope you'll drop in often,' said Clare, seeing Julia down the stairs. 'Anyway, we still have to get together for a lunch, don't we? What about next week?'

'No. Yes. . . I mean. . .' Julia's mind went a complete blank.

'Oh, of course. You'll be flat out at Dawlish next week, won't you?' Clare came to her rescue. 'Never mind, we'll work something out later,' she said cheerfully as Julia hastily got herself into her car. 'Incidentally,' Clare leaned into the window, 'did Richard tell you it was me who suggested he size up

Dawlish as a possible new branch? No?' She took Julia's stunned movement of head as a shake. 'Took all the credit himself, did he? Isn't that just like a man?' Clare laughed, amused, as Julia started the engine, frantic to get away before she gave herself away—burst into tears, or something equally mortifying in front of this friendly, elegant, self-assured woman who was either the epitome of sophistication or as innocent and naïve as Julia herself. Had been.

Or was Clare's disconcerting friendliness prompted by other considerations? Was it a means of telling her how much she needed Richard. . .a subtle, round-about way of asking Julia to leave things be and not to take Richard away from the comfortable established affair that sounded like marriage by any other name—which was what Clare might be hoping it would turn into—perhaps after the children were off her hands? If Richard stayed the distance. If another woman didn't intrude.

As if Julia would! As if she would contemplate snaring Richard away. The thought that she could was fleeting, but nasty none the less. What sort of woman would that make her? Conniving, amoral, desperate. She was none of those awful things; her principles might have taken a battering, but Julia could not envisage the day when she would knowingly be a party to the sort of devious set-up Richard obviously had in mind. Clare would have him all to herself, and welcome, and if she ever did have to share him with another woman that woman was not going to Julia Radcliffe!

The telephone was ringing as Julia let herself into the house. It rang again half an hour later, and then again—and again, as the evening wore on, and each time she just sat there staring at it, visualising Richard at the other end of it. . .the dark, expressive brows peaking into a frown of puzzlement, sharpening into annoyance as he wondered why she wasn't answering. . .wondered where she was.

The last time it rang was going on midnight, and after that Julia went to bed and cried herself to sleep, only to be awakened by more pealing. She reached out to silence the alarm, then realised it hadn't yet gone off and it was the telephone—Richard again, and it was all she could do to stop herself answering and unleashing her rage and hurt at him.

She ignored the ringing several more times, the final time as she was going down the stairs; she heard it as she got the car out, closed the garage door, and then even as she drove off thought she could hear the pealing, or perhaps the sound had just lodged inside her head.

What would Richard think now? That she had not been home all night, of course. Let him, thought Julia with bitter satisfaction, although it was not until Cliff bounded up to her desk shortly after lunch that she realised the groundwork for revenge was already laid in her mind.

'Richard said could you pop upstairs to his office? No, he wasn't due back for another couple of hours, but it seems he can't stay away from the place,' Cliff told her with a laugh as her face registered her surprise and heaven only knew what else.

Forewarned, forearmed, and, nasty jolt over, Julia was quite ready for Richard. She felt reassuringly calm and in control, her anger and hurt gone—or so tightly repressed it made no difference. She didn't need to think how she was going to handle the encounter; she knew.

Richard turned from the window when the secretary showed her in, his face an impassive mask but with a too-bright glitter in his eyes. There was a tightness in the set of the strong, broad shoulders under the pliable fall of expensive material, and for a moment Julia had to fight the image of those shoulders, muscled and bare, and warm to her touch. She thought of Clare Risely and the image vanished.

She met Richard's eyes coolly as she came further into the room, and it seemed outlandish that twenty-four hours ago she had visualised this meeting as a rush into each other's arms. 'Hello, Richard, you're back early. Did you get everything done?' she got in first, blandly pleasant.

Richard ignored the fatuous greeting. 'Where were you last night?' he asked, the impassive mask slipping with the harshness in his voice and giving her a glimpse of the hurt and suspicions he was trying to suppress—playing into her hands, in fact.

Julia furrowed her brow in an exaggerated show of concentration. 'Last night?' she repeated vaguely.

'Last night when I telephoned you. Half a dozen times.'

Eight, she nearly corrected, but kept the spurious perplexed frown in place.

'And this morning, I telephoned again at seven.'

A quarter to, Julia amended in her head, and felt fury gathering willy-nilly inside her. How dared he carry on as if he had a right to find her waiting with bated breath for his calls. . .for those avowals of love that had left her tingling and breathlessly happy, more fool her?

'Oh, that's right. I was out!' she exclaimed as if pleased to have remembered.

'Who with?' Richard demanded, and in spite of himself it sounded like, with the scowl almost a wince.

'Andrew Reith,' Julia lied blandly without a flinch, but her heart starting to race a little with the no-turning-back lie. 'You remember Andrew, don't you? I think you mentioned interviewing him a while ago,' she babbled on easily, with no direction from her brain, while her eyes took note of every flicker of Richard's rapidly changing expression.

'You were out with Reith—all night?' The question carried accusation and incredulity combined.

'That's right,' Julia confirmed lightly. 'We went out and then went back to Andrew's place, and what with one thing and another. . .' She trailed off suggestively, then stepped back in alarm as Richard came across the room at a lunge.

'You spent the night with Reith? I don't believe you,' he rasped, but everything about him told her that he did, and, in spite of having wanted to see that shocked, betrayed expression on his face. . .in spite of hating him, Julia found it hurt that he could believe it of her.

She tried for nonchalance with the shrug and watched him rake agitated fingers through the thick black hair that her own fingers had raked with passion and love. He dropped his hand angrily to his side and stared at her, shaking his head. 'I can't believe it, Julia,' he said despairingly, then flung in with a sort of angry hope, 'You're lying.'

'Why should I?' she tossed back, marvelling at the self-possession that could drive her on to hurt him like this—and enjoy it. Revenge was supposed to be sweet, wasn't it?

'Then what the hell was last Sunday all about?' Richard caught her savagely by the shoulders and literally shook her before flinging her free as if he couldn't bear to touch her any more.

The question had been rhetorical; he was storming back to his desk when her reply stopped him in his tracks. She only said one word: 'Dawlish,' and watched his frozen back with spiteful pleasure in the long, long moment before he turned around, and then, even from the distance that separated them, she could see that the colour had left his face; it was a whitish grey—ashen, and quite ugly, with the skin seeming too tightly stretched over the strong bones of the clamped jaw.

'You know—the managership,' she elaborated unasked, twisting in the knife and suddenly appalled at herself but not able to stop. 'You gave me the job I wanted and. . .' She lifted an airy shoulder '. . . Well, it seemed the least I could do in return.' Had she really said that? She must have, because Richard was coming back to her, slowly, colour returning to his face in a surge of dark, mottled red. He stopped in front of her—close; Julia didn't move as she held his stare.

'You sacrificed your virginity for *that*?' he said quietly, the disbelief tinged by something she recognised as contempt, and all at once she felt as cheap and horrible as she had made herself out to be.

'"Sacrifice" is rather an exaggeration, don't you think? You made it very enjoyable experience.' She gave a vacuous little laugh and thought Richard was going to hit her, and wished he would. . .hit her or shake her—anything to stop the nonsense coming out of her mouth.

'So it was our private ratification of the deal, was it?' The eyes that had loved her short days ago held cold disgust, but still Julia couldn't give in to the protest rising in her throat.

'Something like that,' she returned with shaky bravado, and was frightened by Richard's sudden, nasty laugh.

'You take the cake, Julia Radcliffe.' He shook his head wonderingly. 'You really had me fooled, I'll give you that. The vulnerability. . .the show of outrage when you seemingly thought I wanted favours in exchange for the job. . .then the reluctant softening towards me—all a superb act!' He repeated the nasty grating laugh. 'To think how much time I wasted being careful not to frighten you, pressure; keeping my distance. . .wanting you to like me, trust me, because I thought you had hang-ups about men—sex, when I could have had you in my bed any time. All I'd needed to do, virtually from the moment we met, was assure you that the managership was yours, your career off and running, and you'd have come across at the first opportunity just to ensure I didn't change my mind!'

That was what she had meant him to think, only Julia hadn't allowed for the searing contempt that left her feeling she was gutted by it.

'Were you holding out on old Charles Dawlish

until he came across with the managership?' Richard
jeered through the awful twisted smile. 'And what
about wimp Reith? What's he suddenly acquired to
trade after all this time?'

Julia's hand flew up, but didn't get anywhere near
his cheek. He caught her hand and slammed it down
to her side in a vicious crush of fingers. 'I don't like
being slapped, remember?' he snarled, close to her
face. 'And save the outraged virtue act, you've just
told me what kind of woman you are.'

Julia grappled furiously with his crushing fingers.
'Who the hell do you think you are with your record,
to be acting holier than thou?' she snapped in a
welcome rush of blinding fury. 'Well may you look
surprised,' she taunted as Richard frowned and
relaxed his grip; she tugged her hand free. 'It didn't
occur to you that I'd find out what a low-down, two-
timing creep you are, did it? Mind you, it's no more
than I thought you were, only now I know for
certain, because Clare and I had a very informative
little chat yesterday and——'

'Clare?' Richard fairly yelped the name.

'Clare Risely,' Julia confirmed savagely. 'But don't
worry, I didn't tell her about how you got me into
bed last Sunday, only don't think for a moment that
it was for your sake. It was for Clare's, and what a
nice, decent woman like that is doing having an affair
with a no-good cad like you is beyond me, but by
golly, she can have you!' Richard was looking at her
now as if she had taken leave of her senses, which
quite possibly she had. 'I suppose Clare will be at the
Dawlish launch tonight too?' Julia tossed at him
angrily, and was taken aback by his unexpected,

rather startled nod. 'What did you have in mind? Introducing us and suggesting we be friends, or darting from one to the other and making out you weren't with either of us?' she asked with a cackle of a laugh. 'And don't think I won't be there, because I will—with bells on! Damn it, it's my night, and you're not going to do me out of it! But you can relax; you won't have to carry on as if you're in some French farce, because Andrew Reith is taking me and you can stick to Clare. And then, after tonight, *I'll* decide if I want to stay on at Weldons, and if you dare make one move to get rid of me I'll haul you before every court in the land for wrongful dismissal. . .sexual harassment—oh, I'll think of something, never fear,' she hurled into Richard's dumbstruck face, spun on her heel and flung herself out of the room with a shattering slam of the door.

After all that had happened, it was daft that the only thing on her mind was to get hold of Andrew whom she hadn't seen nor heard from for weeks, and tell him he had to escort her to the Dawlish party. She had told Richard that Andrew was taking her, and, short of sudden death, take her Andrew would. . .must. It would be too mortifying to turn up alone now, the only manager without a partner, and then have Richard ignore her, or worse, parade Clare Risely in front of her nose. Whereas if she didn't go he would think he had shamed her into not being able to show her face, and whatever she might have implied about herself, Julia had nothing to be ashamed about—other than letting herself be taken in by Richard Weldon.

She'd show him! Exactly what, she was in no frame

of mind to work out. Later—tomorrow. . .the next day, she would have to calm down and think things through, but right now she needed to get hold of Andrew, who, infuriatingly, wasn't in the office when she telephoned Fenwick and Jeffcott. Julia left a message for him to return her call, repeating the call and the message several times during the afternoon in between trying to concentrate on the paperwork she needed to finalise for Personnel before the end of the day. In the end, she went home without any word from Andrew, and had no success either when she tried his home number the moment she walked in the door. What now? Going it alone, it looked like.

Propelled by an almost manic energy, Julia threw herself in and out of the shower and into the fabulous white velvet dress. Strapless, skimming her long, lithe form to the top of her knees, it was light years removed from the few dreary after-fives taking up space in her wardrobe, let alone the unexciting collection of practical business outfits; it was the stuff of fashion magazines and romantic fantasies, and Julia didn't care if it was suitable for the occasion or not, or if all the other women were going to be in business clothes or sackcloth and ashes.

She swept her hair into a sleek twist at the back of her head, put on make-up and wondered if she was coming down with the flu; the green eyes glittered feverishly in an unnaturally flushed face which felt hot to the touch as she dabbed on powder to reduce the luminous glow, overdoing the dabs on the upturned tip of the nose and having to waste time dusting it off again. Then she stood back and studied herself. She looked stunning—or at least the dress did. . .sophisticated, remotely beautiful. But what was the point? Richard?

She tried Andrew's number once more, and could have died of relief to finally hear the sound of his voice.

'Andrew! Thank God!' she breathed fervently.

'What is it, Julia? What's happened?' Andrew's voice was full of concern. 'I only got your message at——'

'I can't explain now, Andrew,' Julia cut through his explanation. 'Please just stay where you are. I need you—that is, I need a favour urgently and you must help me. I'll be over in fifteen minutes, all right?'

'Yes, but——'

She hung up without giving him a chance to say anything more. He was home. He could take her. Everything was all right, and she wasn't going to have to slink into her own party alone. She flung on her serviceable beige raincoat over the dress, grabbed her bag and car keys, and ran down the stairs.

Andrew lived in the bottom half of a narrow semi-detached off the Fulham Road, and must have been looking out for her, because he was already opening the front door as she clattered up the short path from the gate.

'For God's sake, Julia, what's happened? Are you all right?' he asked, flicking anxious eyes over her face as if he expected to see blood—bruises, at the very least.

'Fine. I'm fine, I just need a little help, that's all,' Julia assured him with an hysterical little laugh and

tried to get a grip on herself as she followed him
down the hall and into his flat. 'Oh. Hello.' She
pulled up short at the door to the sitting-room and
stared nonplussed at the girl curled up on Andrew's
sofa.

'This is my girlfriend, Lucy; Lucy, this is Julia—an
old colleague of mine—former colleague, I mean,'
Andrew amended his introduction gallantly.

'Hi, Julia,' the girl returned cheerfully. She was
about twenty, blonde and very pretty, and looking at
Julia very curiously.

'Oh,' said Julia weakly, the frenzied panic dying
out of her as she looked back at the only impediment
to Andrew's availability that had not crossed her
mind—a girlfriend.

'What about a drink, and then you can tell me
what it is you need?' Andrew suggested, rising quite
well to the unexpected occasion of having two
women on his hands, one of whom seemed a touch
peculiar.

'Come and sit down,' Lucy invited, obligingly
removing her feet from the sofa to make room.

Julia shook her head agitatedly. 'I can't. I've got to
be at Dawlish at seven-thirty and it's nearly that now.
And I thought—well, I thought you might be able to
take me—come as my partner, I mean,' she blurted,
feeling the heat in her face intensifying into a searing
burn as Andrew stared back amazed.

'Me? Why?'

Why indeed, when the only times she had given
him a passing thought over the last few months was
when Richard dragged up his name out of misplaced

jealousy? 'Because I wanted to arrive with some-body. . .a partner. It's the new branch opening party—my party, Andrew. For Dawlish, you know. . .' A little of her earlier desperation crept back into her voice as she tried to explain without giving herself away.

'But does it matter if you turn up alone? It's only a work affair, isn't it?' His concern gone, Andrew sounded irritable—with reason, Julia supposed, at the interruption to his evening.

'People expect me to come with a partner and I've said. . .well, I've told someone you were bringing me,' she muttered reluctantly, and saw the sudden flash in Lucy's amused eyes.

'It's to do with a man—someone you're keen on; That's it, isn't it?' Lucy pounced to her disconcert-ingly perceptive conclusion with a giggle, and Julia felt so embarrassed she couldn't get away quickly enough.

'It's all right, forget it. Sorry I interrupted you,' she mumbled from the doorway.

'No, wait,' Lucy called her back. 'Of course Andrew can take you. Yes, you can, Andrew,' she insisted to her surprised boyfriend. 'I don't mind.'

It was humiliating to want to accept the proxy offer so desperately. 'I've got my own car, Andrew. We can go separately and then you can leave as soon as. . . Well, as soon as you like.' Julia tried to suppress the pleading from her voice.

'As soon as whoever it is has clapped eyes on you and turned green with jealousy.' Lucy giggled again in undisguised enjoyment. 'Oh, come on, Andrew,' she said impatiently. 'Get your jacket on and be a gentleman for a lady in distress. And I'll come too. It's all right,' she laughed as Julia's face showed horror at the prospect of a threesome. 'I can sit and wait in the car for him—but no longer than half an hour, mind, otherwise I'll have to come in and look for him!'

CHAPTER TEN

LEAVING the car in her old spot behind the building, Julia hurried back to the main street, to find Andrew already waiting impatiently outside Dawlish's spanking-new glass door. She smiled and slipped her hand through his arm in readiness for their grand entrance, felt his arm stiffen and knew he was still annoyed at having been inveigled into escort duty when he had better plans for his evening. Julia couldn't blame him, and was only too grateful to have him at her side in any mood as they entered the premises of Richard Weldon's latest addition to his expanding empire.

She had seen it in its various stages of transformation, but not fully completed. Dawlish was unrecognisable, and Dawlish no longer. With its now uncluttered spaces, elegant screens, lots of expensive pale wood and subtle blue-grey furnishings, it was another world—Weldons, and another time Julia would have been thrilled to be part of it.

They were a little late and there must have already been several dozen people in the front area where once Suzie had reigned idly behind shabby wooden counters. Julia's eyes cut through the throng like butter, alighting almost instantly on Richard's dark head—the back of it, thank goodness—across the room. She couldn't see who he was talking to, but it was not Clare Risely, because Clare was the second

176

person she focused on—a striking figure in cherry-red in the centre of a group some distance from Richard.

'Do you want to take your coat off?' muttered Andrew, a reluctantly solicitous date.

Looking about, Julia saw Eleanor in the 'trusty little black', all sleeves and high neck, Moira in similarly restrained navy, and would have preferred to stay wrapped in her old raincoat all night. 'Yes, why not?' she laughed, letting Andrew help her out of the inelegant coat and hand it to someone whose job it appeared to be to take it. Then Julia plunged forward, like a determined ocean liner, because you couldn't fade into the background in a dress like that, and she hadn't intended to. High exposure was what this night was to be all about—exposure the operative word; Julia was very conscious of dozens of eyes boring into her from all sides, and eventually of Richard's, as he approached, smiling affably, perfectly at ease.

'Ah, the guest of honour. Good evening, Julia.' His eyes swept over her briefly with not a flicker of change in their blandly pleasant expression.

'Hello, Richard. I think you've already met my boyfriend, Andrew Reith.' Julia smiled radiantly and dug her fingers warningly into Andrew's arm to stop any yelp of denial of his new status.

'Glad you could come along, Reith.' Richard shook hands with Andrew, for all the world genuinely pleased to see her 'boyfriend', and Julia couldn't understand it. What had she expected—hoped? Richard turning on Andrew with a snarl? Not quite, but a bit of a glower, or something, and certainly not this smiling, hail-fellow-well-met performance. Julia tried valiantly to maintain the wattage of her own smile.

'There are a lot of people wanting to meet you, Julia; I'll take you around later, but in the meantime do mingle, won't you?' With a nod at both of them, Richard drifted away to do his own mingling, and, smile completely extinguished, Julia stared frowningly after his retreating back.

'Do I take it I've just met the object of this little exercise?' Andrew muttered darkly in her ear.

'Sorry,' she mumbled, distracted, and turned to find Moira at her side, a spruced-up Cyril in tow.

'Julia my dear, you look absolutely beautiful!' Moira looked genuinely impressed, if faintly surprised by so much bare shoulder and so little white velvet beneath, and then frankly curious as she greeted Andrew. 'And Andrew, what a lovely surprise to see you. I didn't know Julia would be bringing you along.'

Neither did Andrew, if Moira but knew.

'Oh, I wanted the opportunity to say a final farewell to Dawlish and the old days,' Andrew returned with a suaveness Julia would not have believed in him. He gave her arm a quick, reassuring little squeeze, and, reassured, she felt some of the umpteen knots of tension unseize inside her stomach.

The conversation turned to 'the old days', to 'do you remembers' and property in general. Safe ground, but Julia could barely listen, let alone participate. Her eyes kept straying. . .watching and waiting, wanting to see them together. Richard and Clare. Perversely, they remained apart, Clare looking very comfortable on her own as she moved about from group to group, and the fact that she didn't appear to feel the need to be at Richard's side was perhaps more telling of the relationship than if she had been clinging to him like a limpet—like Julia herself to Andrew.

Julia abruptly released her grip on his arm at last and took a glass of champagne from a tray proffered by one of the catering staff hired for the occasion. Shortly afterwards, she helped herself to another, and then a third when, his short official speech over, Richard urged them all to drink a toast to the success of the new branch. Julia drank.

'Great, eh?' Cliff joined their little group, introducing the plump pretty woman with him as his wife, Ruth. 'The place looks as if it's been Weldons from time immemorial, doesn't it?' he observed approvingly.

'Doesn't it? And I've always loved Clare's colour schemes,' Ruth put in her bit with the enthusiasm that had to be a family trademark.

Clare's? Julia's glass froze at her lips.

'Clare's?' Moira voiced Julia's own surprise but with innocent curiosity.

'Clare Risely—Richard's sister. She's been responsible for the interiors of all Richard's branches for years,' Cliff explained to Moira. 'Haven't you met her yet?' He cast an eye around the room, located Clare, then gestured. 'That's her over there—in the red.'

'Hmm. Looks very like Richard, doesn't she? And rather familiar. . . Julia, didn't she come here about that house in Chiswell Mews just before you left?'

Moira's voice seemed disembodied and coming from a great distance.

Julia supposed she made some sort of coherent reply, but couldn't be sure. Transfixed, she was staring at Clare as if she had never seen her before. Richard's sister. The same dark hair, same lustrous dark eyes. . .a more delicate, feminine bone-structure, but the likeness was unmistakable. Now. Moira had picked it up at a glance, and Julia might have too, ages ago, if she hadn't been initially side-tracked by the change of location. . .meeting so many new people. Legitimate excuses, but they didn't come near the real reason—the irrational, blinding jealousy which had destroyed her chance of a trusting relationship with Richard.

The chatter and clatter around her had turned into a deafening buzz in her ears, the room was suddenly overwhelmingly stifling, and Julia thought she was going to faint. She looked around in a daze, pushed her empty glass into somebody's hand—Richard's—but didn't stop to wonder how he came to be at her side; she murmured something about fresh air and then was somehow outside and in it, running along the footpath, into the mews and down the lane to her car.

She had fled without her raincoat, and, even once inside the car, was shivering violently with cold and the new shock her nerves were beyond accommodating. The dash through the cold air had cleared her head a little—just enough to make her realise she was in no condition to drive after the three—or was it four?—glasses of champagne on an empty stomach. She fumblingly inserted the key into the ignition so she wouldn't need to rummage for it again, then screamed as the door swung open and an arm reached in and yanked the key out.

'Don't even think it!' Richard bent into the car, and, while her eyes recognised him instantly, her mind took longer to adjust from its blank fright. 'It's me, you idiot,' he reassured her in a growl.

'You frightened me,' Julia found her voice in the accusing whimper of a small child.

'Sorry. Now move over, I'm getting in,' he ordered. 'Come on,' he urged impatiently, giving her a little push to get her moving over the partition between the seats.

With a lot of difficulty and exposed thigh as the slim-fitting dress rode up, Julia hoisted herself into the passenger seat and hastily adjusted the dress as Richard settled into the driver's seat.

'Really, Julia, if you must park in dark alleys, you might at least make sure you lock the door after yourself. I could have been anyone!' he admonished her, the concern sharper than the testiness. 'Here, wrap yourself in this before you freeze to death in that thing.' He had taken off his jacket and was putting it around her cold, bare shoulders, then he switched on the heater for good measure.

'I forgot my coat,' mumbled Julia, huddling into the jacket, its silk lining still warm from Richard's body.

'And your "boyfriend"!' Richard reminded her with a soft laugh. 'He's gone off with his girlfriend, I'm afraid, and, since my sister is obligingly looking after my guests, it leaves us free to have a long-overdue chat, doesn't it? About Clare, for starters. I

take it your whirlwind exit into the night had something to do with my charming sister?'

Was he teasing? Laughing at her? Repressing his
anger until he was ready to unleash it? Julia was not
up to distinguishing nuances. 'Where are we going?'
she asked suspiciously, as Richard turned on the
engine and swung the car out into the lane.

'I'm taking you home.'

She wanted to go home. Huddled into the warm
depths of Richard's jacket, she sat in silence as he
drove them into the main street and past Dawlish, its
lights blazing. . .figures silhouetted against the
blinds. The party was in full swing even without its
host, and the guest of honour, probably not the least
missed, and so much for anybody being
indispensable.

'You should have told me about Clare.' Julia broke
the silence in a small voice, surprising herself with
the edge of truculence, because she had thought that
if ever Richard gave her the opportunity to mention
Clare again she would be bleating apologies for all
the horrible things she had said, implied and thought
about him.

'I thought you knew,' he replied reasonably.

'How could I, when nobody told me?' Julia
demanded pettishly.

'I suppose nobody thought to mention it because
they all assumed you knew—I certainly did,
although not right at the beginning when it was
obvious you hadn't made the connection between
Clare, the mews house and me, and, I have to
confess, I rather enjoyed the novel picture of myself
as the cad setting up his mistress,' Richard admitted

through the dry smile which disappeared almost instantly. 'But believe me, Julia, I had no idea you carried on believing that nonsense. I mean, I saw you myself, talking to Clare, weeks ago.'

'Yes, but I didn't even remember where I'd met her. I didn't have a clue who she really was. And Clare never told me,' Julia added defensively.

'Well, that's hardly surprising, is it?' Richard pointed out very patiently. 'She said you were always dashing past without giving her the chance to talk to you, and anyway, she would have assumed that since *I* was forever talking about you, we'd got down to exchanging the sort of basic information people do—about such mundane things as families and backgrounds. How was she to guess that all we ever did was fight like cat and dog, stopping only long enough to make love?'

'You talked to Clare. . .about me?' Julia felt a fiery wave of humiliation sweep over her.

'Constantly.'

She closed her eyes with the groan. 'Oh God, you didn't tell her that I. . .'

'For Pete's sake, what do you take me for?' Richard snapped peevishly. 'No, don't answer that; you already told me this afternoon.'

Julia bit hard into her lower lip to stop the cry of protest. 'I didn't mean them, Richard—those awful things I said,' she said barely above a whisper.

'Didn't you?' he challenged, keeping his eyes on the road ahead and refusing to turn to meet the appeal in her gaze. 'Did you actually make love with me last Sunday while believing I was involved with another woman?' he asked suddenly after a pause that had extended for the best part of a block.

Julia shook her head mutely, then realised he couldn't see the silent answer. 'No. I didn't think anything like that any more, which is why it was such a shock when I saw Clare in Chiswell Mews on Thursday and it all came back and I thought that you. . . I would never have—you know. . .if I'd known. . .thought. . .' she trailed off lamely, entangled in a sea of incoherence and sentences she didn't know how to finish.

'Wouldn't you?'

Was the voice pleased or disappointed? 'No, of course not!' she said, shocked. 'I don't think so,' she amended the heated denial in a mumbled afterthought because nothing was clear-cut any more, least of all her principles. How could she tell what she would or would not have done if they had really been put to the test? Yes, in the heat and hurt of her 'discovery' she had convinced herself she never wanted to see Richard again, but then what was the afternoon and evening's frenzied behaviour all about? The need to parade poor old Andrew. . .? The desperate need to make Richard jealous? Deep down, Julia knew the answer; she wanted Richard no matter what. . .would shut her eyes to half a dozen other women in his life if she had to, just to be part of that life.

They had arrived at her house. Julia looked on dully as Richard got out to open the garage door, and stayed seated, locked in her miserable thoughts, after he had driven them into the garage and closed the door again. He would call a taxi the moment they got upstairs and then return to the party, and that would be that; she would never be alone with him again—if he could help it.

'Are you planning to spend the night in there?' he said impatiently as he held the car door open for her.

Julia emerged reluctantly from the dark, warm cocoon, and they went into the hall and up the stairs like a dreary married couple returning from a not-very-successful night out—not talking because there was nothing to say that hadn't been said to death already.

'The telephone's over there.' She pointed to the instrument on the dresser in the dining alcove. 'So you can ring for the taxi,' she added in reply to Richard's blank look. 'You want to get back to your party, don't you?'

'No, I do not want to get back to my party.' His face was taut like his voice, and the dark eyes alive with an anger that sent a strange thrill through her and a rush of too many contradictory feelings to distinguish one from another. 'We're going to talk, Julia, and I'm not leaving until we've thrashed everything out once and for all. We may have sorted out Clare, but we haven't touched base yet, have we? What about us, Julia? What about *me*?' Richard demanded harshly, suddenly reaching to her. . .wanting to touch her, if only to shake her, but dropped his hand again and just stared, glared, at her. 'I need to know how you feel about me, Julia, because I can't stand not knowing any longer. I've had two hair-tearing months worrying if I'm coming on too strong or not strong enough—terrified I might send you and your precious career flying back behind that barricade never to be seen or heard of again.'

'My "precious career" happens to be very important to me.' Scared, under threat from the moment of truth she sensed was around the corner, Julia struck out with the old knee-jerk response before she could stop herself.

'So important you slept with me to advance it?'

She jerked back as if he had slapped her, and the quiet, bitter words hurt more than if he had. She stared at him in horror. They had 'touched base,' she recognised that in a slow trickle of comprehension; she understood now why hypothetical mistresses were so much water off a duck's back; real or imagined, they paled into insignificance beside the dreadful suspicion Richard must have been carrying about with him since she had hurled the ultimate insult at him this afternoon.

'No! No, Richard, no.' She shook her head wildly and kept on shaking it as if she had forgotten she was doing it. 'I lied. I was hurt and angry and I wanted to hurt you. You can't believe I meant it, Richard, you can't!'

He gave an abrupt shrug that was a sort of belligerent, unwilling capitulation. 'So help me, Julia, I don't know what to believe when you carry on as if your work is the only thing that matters to you,' he said wearily. 'Mine's important to me too, not least for the independence it brings me, and I can understand you—anybody, man or woman—wanting that, and I'd help you all I could to get ahead, help you set up your own business when you were ready. But, Julia, career and independence are not the be-all and end-all of existence, and success can be pretty hollow if there isn't anyone to share it with you. I want to share mine with you, plus all the simple, ordinary things money can't buy, and last Sunday I thought— hoped—that you'd finally admitted to yourself that you wanted me in your life as much as I want you in mine. But then this afternoon when you. . .'

Julia saw the doubt and pain in his eyes and couldn't let him finish. She moved to him, took both his hands and tried to wrap his arms around herself, and it seemed an age before he complied and drew her against himself, his hands locking around her under the jacket she had forgotten she was still wearing.

'Oh, I do want you, Richard, I do!' she assured him vehemently. 'I love you. I want to make love with you again. I want an affair with you for as long as you want,' she added, and what more could she say to reassure him that he hadn't been mistaken. . .that she wanted him in her life for as long as he wanted to stay in it? She stared up into his eyes, waiting for relief to replace the doubt, for their dark depths to light up with pleasure and his arms tighten crushingly in the embrace her body ached for.

'An affair?' Richard's light embrace slackened and then wasn't there at all; nor did his surprise carry any relief or pleasure in it. 'Is that what you want?'

Julia nodded slowly. 'Don't you?' she asked uncertainly.

'You love me enough to have an affair with me. Well, that's something.' He gave a sudden, unamused laugh.

Perplexed, she watched him wander distractedly to the window at the other end of the room and stand there with his back to her, staring out through the still-undrawn curtains. What had she said wrong now? Dear God, she loved him. She had admitted that to him at last and without reservations. . .asked for no commitment, no guarantees. What more did he want from her?

Richard turned and seemed to have aged ten years; the sag along the shoulders hadn't been there a moment ago. 'So you don't trust me after all,' he said in a bitter conclusion which hurt all the more because Julia couldn't fathom its cause. 'All men are not like your father, Julia. Sure, thousands of men desert their wives and kids, but a hell of a lot don't,' he pointed out with a spurt of anger, and she had to do a mental somersault to adjust to this new subject from nowhere.

'I know,' she agreed, puzzled.

'Then why won't you trust me enough to marry me?'

'Marry you?' she mouthed, stunned.

'Yes, marry me. I'm not into affairs, Julia—thank you for the offer,' Richard threw in with sarcastic courtesy. 'I never have been, and I——' Her amazement finally seemed to register with him. He was across the room in the time it took her to mouth the word 'marry' again. 'What did you think I was talking about? An affair?'

Julia nodded.

'Oh God!' He started to laugh, then cut off the unamused, jarring sound with equally jarring abruptness. 'I didn't mention the actual word, did I?'

She shook her head.

'An unpardonable oversight—forgive me. Darling, I want you to marry me. Is that clear enough now?' He was being—trying to be—facetious, but the desperate hope in his eyes gave him away. He was still as unsure of her as she was of him. Of herself.

'Why?' Julia asked in a small, clear voice.

'Why what?'

'Why do you want to marry me? You don't have to. I mean, just because we slept together. . .' How gauche and naïve that sounded! Julia had stopped even before Richard had let out a growl of exasperation.

'Can't you understand?' he demanded despairingly. 'I love you. I fell in love with you the moment we met and I want to marry you for a hundred and one reasons—not all of them fit for delicate ears, but which I shall enumerate one by one if you give me the chance. Later. Right now, I want to hear just one word from you. "Yes" or "no", Julia?' he asked huskily.

He was asking for an answer to a host of questions. . .did she love him enough? Trust him enough? Want him enough to take the risk she had been so terrified of for so long? And amazingly they could all be answered with the same small word.

Julia was nodding long before she managed to get the word out, and, already gathered up into his arms, with Richard's mouth impatient to claim her, she could only murmur the, 'Yes. Yes. Yes!' against his lips.

'That was three words,' Richard murmured back. 'And I loved every one of them.'

1992

Celebrate the most romantic day of the year with
MY VALENTINE 1992—a sexy new collection of four
romantic stories written by our famous Temptation
authors:

**GINA WILKINS
KRISTINE ROLOFSON
JOANN ROSS
VICKI LEWIS THOMPSON**

My Valentine 1992—an exquisite escape into a romantic
and sensuous world.

Don't miss these sexy stories, available in February at your favorite retail outlet. Or order your
copy now by sending your name, address, zip or postal code, along with a check or money
order for $4.99 (please do not send cash) plus 75¢ postage and handling ($1.00 in Canada),
payable to Harlequin Books to:

In the U.S.
3010 Walden Avenue
P.O. Box 1396
Buffalo, NY 14269-1396

In Canada
P.O. Box 609
Fort Erie, Ontario
L2A 5X3

Please specify book title with your order.
Canadian residents add applicable federal and provincial taxes.

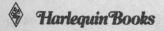

Harlequin Books

VAL-92-R

HARLEQUIN
PROUDLY PRESENTS
A DAZZLING NEW CONCEPT IN ROMANCE FICTION

One small town—twelve terrific love stories

Welcome to Tyler, Wisconsin—a town full of people
you'll enjoy getting to know, memorable friends and
unforgettable lovers, and a long-buried secret that
lurks beneath its serene surface....

JOIN US FOR A YEAR IN THE LIFE OF TYLER

Each book set in Tyler is a self-contained love story;
together, the twelve novels stitch the fabric of a
community.

LOSE YOUR HEART TO TYLER!

The excitement begins in March 1992, with
WHIRLWIND, by Nancy Martin. When lively, brash
Liza Baron arrives home unexpectedly, she moves
into the old family lodge, where the silent and
mysterious Cliff Forrester has been living in seclusion
for years....

WATCH FOR ALL TWELVE BOOKS OF THE TYLER SERIES
Available wherever Harlequin books are sold

Janet Dailey
Americana

A romantic tour of America through fifty favorite Harlequin Presents novels, each one set in a different state, and researched by Janet and her husband, Bill. A journey of a lifetime in one cherished collection.

Don't miss the romantic stories set in these states:

March titles #27 NEBRASKA
Boss Man from Ogallala

#28 NEVADA
Reilly's Woman

April titles #29 NEW HAMPSHIRE
Heart of Stone

#30 NEW JERSEY
One of the Boys

Available wherever
Harlequin books are sold.